Ancestry

John Simmons Short Fiction Award

Ancestry

Eileen O'Leary

University of Iowa Press · Iowa City

University of Iowa Press, Iowa City 52242
Copyright © 2020 by Eileen O'Leary
www.uipress.uiowa.edu
Printed in the United States of America
Text design by Sara T. Sauers
Cover design and illustration by Derek Thornton, Notch Design

Printed on acid-free paper

Library of Congress Cataloging-in-Publication Data
Names: O'Leary, Eileen (Eileen Kelly), 1946–author.
Title: Ancestry / Eileen O'Leary.
Description: Iowa City: University of Iowa Press, [2020] |
    Series: John Simmons Short Fiction Award
Identifiers: LCCN 2020006512 (print) |
    LCCN 2020006513 (ebook) |
    ISBN 9781609387426 (paperback; acid-free paper) |
    ISBN 9781609387433 (ebook)
Classification: LCC PS3615.L4285 A6 2020 (print) |
    LCC PS3615.L4285 (ebook) |
    DDC 813/.6—dc23
LC record available at https://lccn.loc.gov/2020006512
LC ebook record available at https://lccn.loc.gov/2020006513

"Tid" was published in the *Black Fork Review*, no. 1, 2019.
"Michigan Would Get Beautiful" was published in *Qu*, May 2020.

Dedicated to the memory of Lois Ahfterdahl

Contents

Ancestry

Tid

I CAME UP FROM the basement at Vesterhoff's and noticed in the biggest of the viewing rooms everyone was on the floor, on their stomachs no less and with their arms extended forward. There's not a sound. The bier and the flowers under the lights, and here's this worship going on. What religion was this? All the years I've been working for funeral parlors, and I'd never seen anything like it. The next day, I ran into Vesterhoff, and he told me I'd walked past an armed robbery.

I was telling this to the great-uncle of the girl who just married my son. Once the reception started, he came over to talk to me. He told me he'd never met a freelance embalmer before.

"There you are," I said. "A profession of excitement and danger."

I retain some Norwegian accent even after living in America all these years, and the next thing the man says is how much he'd like a Viking funeral. I hear this sort of thing a lot. The body on a boat and the boat, on fire, sent off toward the horizon.

He said, "But I'm sure it's not allowed. Everything is restricted now."

"Of course you can do it," I told him. "Almost anything is possible to arrange. You'd want to plan ahead, though. Maybe even have the boat and a gallon of pitch ready. And a large brush to get the pitch all over yourself. Hire someone who'd be able to shoot a flaming arrow into the boat as it takes off with you. Don't leave all that to your family. It could turn your funeral into a scavenger hunt."

Now he suspects I'm having him on. He turns and moves toward my wife on the other side of the table. I'd put him past ninety. One of Dad's pending customers, as my children would call him. Old as he is, the dream of a Viking funeral doesn't appear to be something he considers imminent.

It's a big wedding, our youngest son, Dan, and Carmen. They say a man always marries his mother. My own mother died when I was young, and I retain only a slight memory of her, but I believe there's some truth to this. You might think Carmen, who's short and dark, couldn't be less like Laura, who is very tall and ginger-haired, but they're both in the travel business, and Carmen tells the same kind of long, involved stories that Laura does. My wife is the Tolstoy of anecdotists.

Dan, in the meantime, looks and sounds like my father. His voice can unnerve me over the phone or if I'm hearing him from a different room.

My father's voice, soft and full of hesitations, was not a lecturer's voice, though lecture is what comes to mind when I recall him. He had a tendency to instruct. He studied Norwegian history, prehistory in fact, the first peoples after the ice age. He had been preparing for museum work when the Nazis invaded Norway during World War II. Everything, pleasure and complaint, changed to become something it wasn't or disappeared. His city was bombed. He ended up with my mother's family. They owned a small farm way out in the country. It's where I was born. When Laura later described it, she used the word *picturesque*. This was kindness.

My father wasn't made for farming. He was a perfectionist. "Nature needs to be messy," he'd tell me. Of the work we did, the messiest seemed to be when we'd be up all night helping the cows giving birth in spring. I say "spring" with levity. The weather could be terrible. For their survival, the newborns were kept in the dark barn, where they stayed dry and out of the wind. When it was truly summer, my father waited until my sister and I could join him before he'd say, "*Tid*," the word for "time." Then we'd open the door, and one by one, these young animals walked out into sunlight, first with shyness, and then, to our delight, they'd begin leaping and gamboling and spinning, very joyful at the shock of seeing the world. The tone of his voice when he said "*Tid*" was the closest I've come to religion.

His lost chance at working in a museum stayed on his mind. I can't remember a time he wasn't telling me about the very first of us, a time so far back I couldn't imagine it. The ice covering the country had receded, revealing land. People came up from the south.

"In boats?" I'd ask.

"Boats that they'd made by hand. They watched the ice unlock the sea. They finished their boats and set off. In a world of dark water, they see some green ahead. The boats thump onto shore. You can imagine the first footprint. Then another."

"What did they say?"

"Ha ha. HA HA HA."

"Does that mean hello?"

"It means ha HA! Why would they say hello? There was nobody there."

He'd describe stone tools. He'd ask me what I thought those people used for shelter. I should someday have the museum apprenticeship he'd missed. But there was none to be had. I recall him at the table, helping me write letters, telling me we'd find something. A position that would support me. One particular afternoon, when word came that another possibility had failed, he lost his temper and went out into the late sunlight, hollering at the sky.

When he finally prevailed on some friend of a neighbor's relative—in Malmö, Sweden, yet—to bring me on, it was in the funeral business, and we both had a good laugh at that.

"There's a living in death?"

"How much of a living should the dead give?"

But the man to whom I was apprenticed disliked Norwegians. Or he simply disliked me. It seemed he wanted someone who appreciated his practical jokes. He saw himself as a kind of character, a celebrity even in his tiny corner of the world.

I was painfully homesick. And in a form of homesickness, I experienced my late mother's voice returning vividly to my memory. It was as though she were speaking at my ear—her high, phlegmy voice full of music. Cholly? Almost three syllables to say Charlie. As though she were again calling me to her. Cholly? The first time I heard her in my head like that, I had to sit down.

Not long into my apprenticeship, while reading instructions for how to calculate the solution to the size and weight of the body, I felt a sharp sudden pain at the back of my head. The man had struck me. I told him not to do that. I was very careful when I said this because I couldn't lose this position. At the very least, my father would be devastated. My instinct was to hit back, but a further instinct believed this was what he wanted, a reason to toss me out. I wouldn't give that to him. But I was afraid if I said nothing, he might begin doing worse. He complained that I was morbid, and this was a burden to him.

"I have enough dead people as it is," he said to me. "You look too serious."

He was obligated by contract to teach me. Beyond that, he wouldn't talk to me.

The strange thing was that I was capable of being very lighthearted. But I could hardly then begin showing that side of me. And he was no one whose company I could enjoy. So I became increasingly depressed, which only supported the man's opinion of me. Being myself around him was impossible. In addition to being hit, I felt as though I didn't quite exist. I couldn't say which sensation was worse.

For relief, I would head out every single night to the bar and a table with friends. I was there when a tall, pretty girl walked in. My friends hailed her to join us. She was on vacation, she told us, checking out the planet. This was Laura. Lawwa. From New Yawk. We teased her about her accent. This allowed us to hide our reaction to her body. I moved as close to her as I could, but the competition for her had already begun.

She came back the following night. Touring around like a nut, she told us, and I'm dying for a good beer. A good beeya.

Everything seemed to happen to her. Joining us in the evening, she'd have encountered something earlier that we were not going to believe. Her world was full of people who told her the most amazing things. Wait'll you hear. These same people we would have passed on the street earlier without noticing them. I don't believe she ever finished a glass before taking off again and leaving us to miss her. We were all in love with her.

The bride's great-uncle isn't able to talk with Laura because of the two grandchildren crawling over her shoulders and head. He nods a farewell and dodders over to where he'd been aiming himself all along. Annette, our second child. He's introducing himself to her like some swain, some young stud. Good God. At his age.

Annette is more than a match for him, diplomatically speaking. She works in public relations. She has sent worse cases on their way with a look of contentment. It's the same thing you do, Daddy, only mine are breathing.

But to see him up on his toes and fairly blushing. Not about to go gently is he. And not much time left before he lands on a cold metal table. I imagine him, as I did almost daily my apprentice instructor. I would be wearing my gown and face protector, the apron, gloves— haute hazmat. I'd cut near the collarbone and find his carotid and the internal jugular, nip in and connect the machine to each. Scrub him down hard to send the solution through him. It is astonishing how fresh and rejuvenated the skin looks with the infiltration of embalming fluid.

There, Annette has talked him around to face in the other direction, and he's looking for his wife and his empty chair. Now I realize Charlie, our eldest, standing with his glass raised, a microphone in the other hand, has managed to alert the room to the little scene. Everyone's watching the great-uncle make his way over to his table as though he's still a young man, vital. I find I like him.

Charlie's voice comes over the amplifiers. You would call his personality eerily calm. He works with a science foundation studying deep-space. They consider what the earth will be like a million years from now.

"Everything we take for granted will be completely different."

"Everything?"

"The only thing you'll recognize is the sound of laughing."

During my apprenticeship, one of the friends I'd made, who'd just finished medical training, took me to view an autopsy. He was at a hospital not far from me, instructing students, and enabled me to join the group. That afternoon, I was given more than just the slight window my work gives me into a human body. I'd studied anatomy, and I'd seen charts depicting the human interior, but nothing came close to this. The entire torso was opened wide.

Describing it to Laura, I compared it to pictures from a reef where the colors and shapes below the ocean were a great surprise. Or the shock of seeing photographs from outer space, which I hadn't realized would have colors. I just hadn't considered what was really there. The skin is something of a liar. Inside, everything is very bright, jewellike, the gall-bladder of all things. My medical friend was aware of what I was going through with the apprenticeship.

I told Laura this back when she had again joined us one evening. I wanted something to happen. She was sitting across from me. I waited until she'd finished describing the amazing occurrence she'd experienced earlier; crossing the street for this woman was epic. Anyway, I told her I had been to the hospital that day.

She looked stricken.

"Not as a patient," I'd said and told her the reason I'd been there. I described the colors, the brightness inside the body.

She leaned forward, studying my face. It was that moment that I believed I had a chance with her. She was taking that measure that women do, that millisecond in the eye, the calculation. "Hold on," she said. "Wait. To cheer you up, he took you to an autopsy?"

I've heard her retell this story. Most of what she remembered, I hadn't noticed that night. She included descriptions of my friends around the table, and I had never before realized how peculiar each was.

Anyway, that was the beginning. A very long time ago. A small wedding in Malmö. Then the children came. I see myself for many years half-dressed and running toward anyone crying. It didn't seem that either of us had time to think. Then they left. When the first grandchild was born, Laura told me we were back in business. I will be dead in one year, though I was told months, six, possibly seven. The same thing that took my father.

My sister is sitting near Laura and doing a stoic, sympathy kind of thing with her clenched jaw, and I wish she and my silent brother-in-law were less grim. Just as well. At their best, they're a complaining, suffering pair, always with a remark to belittle. I'm surprised they showed up.

"They're only here to see if I've become some sort of wreck," I told Laura when we were getting dressed. "So they can wallow in it. So they can say, 'Oh. He's become a shadow of himself.' It's the only way they'll ever like me. They hope I'm miserable."

"Disappoint them."

I have made no plans for a Viking funeral. I've made no plans at all. I will be distracting myself up to the very end of it. My father was like that. After I was finished with my apprenticeship and had a job—a good one with good people—I went home during a February when he was at the very end. He told me his intentions for the garden that summer while we both understood he had only a few days left. He gave detailed and specific plans for the peas, "*erter*," as he would have called them. The tomatoes he wouldn't plant in the same place, as they take too much from the soil. He was deciding where he'd put them.

I think his voice held the reason for the phenomenon that I experienced later that night. When I went up to bed, I was struck by how safe I felt in my father's house. Here I was, a young man, tall, and fairly strong, while my father could hardly move, could hardly breathe, yet I was certain that whatever trouble came through the door, however frightening, it would be my father rising up and protecting me.

I wonder if our children, when they're home, which they are often enough, do they enjoy the same delusion? Do they share the sense of safety that I took from my father until his last breath when I became a reliquary of his voice, everything I heard him say, from "Ha ha" up to and including how best to stake the peas and where to plant the tomatoes?

Michigan Would Get Beautiful

RODGE WAS NOT a hurrying kind of guy, but he moved quickly when the front doorbell kept ringing like an alarm.

Cecile hurried in. "I had to hit the bell with my elbow. My God."

Rodge got the box of Band-Aids and soon was covering the blisters at the base of his wife's thumbs, along her fingers, over her palms.

"Ow," she said and then laughed to reassure him. "The staple gun tried to kill me."

"You need to hire an assistant."

"It's only one room."

"If you can't get help, you should quit the whole idea," he said.

She laughed at him.

"Look at your hands."

"They will heal."

"I mean it." He worked for a hospital in accounts receivables and his world was full of people who ended up in the ER, sometimes dying because of preventable accidents. "I'm telling you to stop. I insist."

"No."

The Jordan house—the Jordan room, and a small room at that—was her first job. She didn't have enough money to hire an assistant, not after living off her savings while she learned the interior decorating business.

It was not lost on him that as soon as their wedding was over, Cecile had begun redecorating him. But he'd been flattered, really. His coworkers noticed him all of a sudden. And Cecile's concern for the right cut and collars of his shirts—well, it had been fun to get so much attention. But now she was all about the Jordans. The way the Jordans lived. How everything about the Jordans was just right.

"And when they don't pay you? How will you like the Jordans then?"

"They gave me a deposit," she said, her voice rising. "Of course they'll pay the rest."

That night, he couldn't get near her with her hands swollen and balanced over her crotch like a fence. He went out to the living room and sat alone in front of the TV, cracking open a beer and staring at a sports channel. This had been his life before meeting Cecile. He didn't want it back.

Cecile Collette had been Pat Graves before she decided to quit her office management job and follow her passion, a financially dangerous move. "It's now or never," she told her coworkers who'd gently implied she was out of her mind. She was forty-nine. This was in Pittsburgh. She moved to Cleveland. It was only two hours west, but it was somewhere else. She wanted nothing around her to lull her back to old routines. Everything would be new, including her name.

Since she was changing her life, she decided to dip her toe—might the ice have finally melted?—into the waters of love. She joined online dating sites, one of which coughed up Roger "Rodge" Debrett, only two years her junior, who professed to liking candlelight and long walks in the rain—bogus she was sure—but whose mint green shirt with dark-green stitching, epaulets, and white buttons cried out to her for rescue.

They met for coffee. He talked a lot about himself, but she ignored his sales pitch. Rather, she was assessing his comb-over, the fit of his jacket, the possibility he'd inflated his value. And had there been damage in his early years? Yes, she thought, I could do something with him.

Naked and spread-eagled, she listened, shocked, to her loud and un-controllable giggling—she *giggled*?

Rodge hopped in circles, his lowering hard-on bobbing up and down, his tie over his hair like a headband while he cried, "Hoo ah! Hoo ah! Hoo ah!"

It was during their honeymoon—two nights at the Renaissance-Marriott with a pair of tickets to a Browns game and dinner at Johnny's —that he noticed how she'd touch every fabric she came close to. It made him think of Braille.

"Isn't it all just cotton?" he'd joked, listening to her identify what the bedspread was, what the thread count was, what the pillows were expected to do. A cold look came into her eye, and he hurriedly back-tracked and let her know he was actually "pretty bowled over." Hell, she had to realize, he told her, "I don't know any of that stuff."

Her eyes remained steady. "I don't want you to know it," she said. "It's only important that I know it. It's what I *do*."

"Well," he smiled a certain smile, "as long as it's not all you do."

In the morning, Cecile let herself into the Jordan house, a rambling clapboard in Cleveland Heights, big as far as she was concerned, but lacking the reach and manicured lawns of wealthier neighborhoods. Inside was a mix of valuable and worthless pieces and, like place-savers, possessions of the two children who were off at college. There were also toys for the toddler, a late baby, Poppy.

Hallie Jordan told Cecile she'd called her after seeing her ad in the church bulletin. Which church Hallie meant would remain a mystery; Cecile had joined three. Possible clients would connect Cecile Collette Designs with the fellow parishioner seen in a (Presbyterian, Episcopalian, Catholic) pew. She had also joined the Rotary, the Mandel Community Center, the Chamber of Commerce, and two book groups. All this in addition to her website and a blog.

And only the Jordan room to show for it. Cecile learned that the problem with following a passion late in life was muscling onto the turf of people who'd followed *their* passion a whole lot earlier. She was gently but unequivocally rejected for hire in their shops. Her competition was not only dug in but fiercely defensive. She was an unattended nova in a very small heaven.

"Cecile," Hallie cried as she came into the kitchen. She was carrying Poppy. The little girl had Down syndrome, and her wide face held a questioning look as she turned to Cecile.

"Hi, you two."

"No, what happened to your hands?"

"Nothing. They're fine. Comes with the territory. Hello, Poppy. Hello."

The child tucked her head into her mother's neck.

Turning to find her purse and car keys, Hallie said, "I may not be back before you leave. Help yourself to coffee, okay?"

When they'd gone, Cecile felt that icy freedom of being alone in someone else's house. Quietly, almost on tiptoe, she walked through the first floor. Framed photos covered the walls of the hallway. Smiling Jordans. The two older kids holding Poppy between them like a prize. Troy Jordan in a summer chair, mugging in Ray-Bans. The fact that no one was breathing or speaking in the pictures encouraged her to idealize their lives. She studied the progress of the older two, from baby photos through school years and into young adulthood, taking them into her heart until she might have given birth to them herself. She returned to her work in a confusion of moods: inspired, sad, motherly, joyful, even elegiac, having lived through a generation of a family in a concentrated twenty minutes.

The problem she'd been solving for Hallie was a room off the kitchen. It was too big and too open to be made into a pantry, and the lack of windows made it difficult for any other use. Cecile drew up a picture of the room as a breakfast nook inside a tent, pleated fabric covering the ceiling and walls, light fixtures that were simple and strategically set.

Hallie hadn't been sure of hiring her until she'd seen the drawing. "You can do this?"

Outlining the room in furring strips had been easy. Getting the pleating around the central point of the ceiling had gone well. Tall, she was also strong and not afraid of ladders. But using the staple gun became an issue. By the time she attached the fabric along the top of the walls, she could barely move her hands. A hammer and tacks worked until she smashed a fingernail.

She decided to spend the morning trimming and taping the fabric edges. After methodically working around the little room, she found her fingertips drying out and splitting. Moisturizer would help, but it might stain the fabric. In her tool bag she had a box of disposable latex gloves. She put on a pair and continued.

That night, with her hands throbbing anew, she began to think she hadn't asked enough for the job. She'd been afraid to lose the business if she asked for more money. Wasn't an initial low price better? But the room was turning out amazing.

"What's wrong with you?"

"Sorry. Nothing's wrong, Rodge. Go back to sleep."

She wanted to kill herself for not asking enough money. There were guidelines. Why hadn't she followed them? Well, she hadn't, and that was that. What she needed were more clients, which raised another question. What was keeping her from making Hallie her friend? They were about the same age. Going over the short conversations they'd had, it seemed as if Hallie was offering friendship. But that could be courtesy. A presumption on Cecile's part could be damning for future business. But if they became friends, Cecile could connect to Hallie's other friends and then the friends of those friends.

"Quit sighing."

"Sorry."

"What's the matter?"

"Nothing."

"How about we do it?"

"What? Oh. My hands."

"Are we ever going to do it?"

"Of course, but my—"

"We can do it without using your hands."

"Rodge, it's pretty late."

"Don't move. Okay? I'll do everything."

"But I need you to get me turned on first."

"I know. That's what I'm doing."

"It's not really—Rodge."

"Keep your hands in the air."

"It's not—"

"What!" he yelled. "It's not what? There's always something that—this started with the Jordans. You have to get away from that snob crowd. It's them!"

She threw back the covers and hurried out to the living room.

Rodge followed, yelling. "The damn Jordans, damn, rich Jordans. You have to stop this stupid stuff, Cecile."

Cecile now began seeing Rodge as she would a large, unmovable cabinet that drew the eye from the rest of an otherwise beautiful room.

He yelled.

She shoved him toward the front door.

He yelled louder.

"I need my sleep," she screamed, "so I can do a good job for the Jordans. It'll get me more work."

It was the following day when the trouble started. After Hallie settled Poppy in for an afternoon nap, she saw Troy getting out of his car. His face looked damaged. "How come you're home?"

"Can you come inside?" he asked and let her lead the way into the house. "Is that woman here?"

"No. She's picking up a light fixture. She'll be back."

"Christ."

He went into the living room and sat down, waiting until she sat across from him. "First thing this morning, because we're getting backed up, I call the outfit making the new machine."

"For the eco bags."

"Yep. I say, 'Hello. It's Troy Jordan. I'm checking on the order.' And he says, 'What order?'"

"He lost your order?"

"There was no order. He never got an order. No deposit, no nothing."

"So you reordered?"

"With what? There's no money. That shit took the loan money. My partner."

She stared at him, picturing his partner's friendly, undistinguished face. "He took it where?"

"He stole it. He'd been out for a week, so this morning, I call up the machine people. 'How's it hangin'?' I find out nothing's hanging. So I start checking. He cashed out our line of credit. I don't know where he went. He'd put in for vacation. I thought he was in Wyoming."

"Wait. He took the money for himself?"

"I was with the lawyers for two hours before I had to get out of there. That shit left with over three million dollars, and I have to pay it all back, which I can't, and no machine, no way to fill the new orders. No nothing. We've been backed up with shipments and getting the place up to speed for the new stuff."

"There must be papers. Contracts."

"Oh there were, yeah. I signed all sorts of papers. They were dummy papers. Nothing was real. I called in the lawyers. They called the prosecutor and the FBI. Jesus Christ. Everything."

"God."

"I trusted him."

"Was he on drugs?"

"I don't know."

"Or gambling."

"I don't know."

"What about insurance? Is there insurance?"

"Nothing that stops the bank from taking the business. They'll take everything. Or they'll give me another loan, and I'm not sure I can manage two of them."

"He'll be found. You can't disappear anymore."

"I'll never see that money though. And I may be sued. I may be indicted. I don't know what legal costs I'm looking at. The payroll still has to get out. This morning I thought that machine we ordered, *thought* we ordered—I was worried about the ventilation and the electrical codes—and this son of a bitch—"

"Legal costs? They can't indict you."

"You know what's funny? He knew just when we had the most cash available to cover everything. I was at the table making plans with this shit, and all the time, he's waiting for everything to ripen."

Hallie was silent, staring at Troy, who now flung himself up and against the back of the chair as though the thing had goosed him. She only stared at him for something to focus her eyes on while this news shifted and butted inside her head. She began thinking very quickly.

The cars, she could sell one of the cars and a lot of the furniture, most of it, and sell the house, the contents of their life suddenly flying off into the blue.

It came to her that she would never want to eat anything ever again. What'll we do? seemed a question both inadequate and redundant to the moment. After a long time—sunlight slipping from the front of the house to the back, the middle of the day leaving them with the beginning of an afternoon—the news was no longer something that happened to other people. Never to them.

He said, "We tell the kids the rest of college is their dime. They'll be all right." Seeing her face, he said, "They will be."

"I know."

"I wish I was younger. For what's coming. I'm thinking of driving off a bridge."

"Don't drive off a bridge."

"Okay."

Poppy. Security for Poppy. Now something violent squeezed her heart. She felt herself trembling.

He said, "Off a cliff?"

"No."

"I think I'm serious."

"Please."

A slow creaking noise came to them. Cecile was letting herself in through the back door. There followed a long struggling sound as though she might be burdened with a large package. The noise became a scrabbling. Then the quick suction of her shoes—was she trying to be quiet? The kitchen might have been the aim of an inept burglar. Had someone else decided to rob them? One thief wasn't enough? They got two?

Catching her husband's eye, Hallie's shoulders began to shake. Troy threw up his hands. He began shaking, too, his eyes shut, his mouth opened wide, gasping back laughter. After a short time, hysteria played out only to return when they heard Cecile call out to them from the kitchen, "I'm here?"

"Okay," Hallie managed to answer before leaning sideways against the sofa arm, her eyes squeezed shut, shaking with strangled laughter. Grief seized up inside her. "Oh," she said finally, sniffing, sighing. Pointing toward the kitchen, she whispered, "That room might make it easier to sell the house, the—decor?" She was gripped again in hysteria, tears down her face and her breathing hiccupping.

That evening when Rodge came home from work, Cecile was soaking her hands in Epsom salts. He found the ibuprofen and fed two pills into her mouth and held a glass of water gently against her lower lip so she could swallow them.

"He was home in the afternoon," Cecile told Rodge. "Troy. I heard them laughing in the living room. I was hanging the chandelier. It's not a real chandelier. It's plain. But it was just big enough and just heavy enough. Thought I'd fall off the ladder. And don't look at me like that. I can hang lights. It was just. . . . They were laughing. You know how people make those wheezing, sucking sounds like they're trying to be quiet, but they can't stop laughing?" She felt close to tears, hurt by the suspicion they'd been laughing at her.

What she didn't tell Rodge was what followed the laughing. There was a long moment of silence, and then Cecile realized they'd moved to the living room floor and were having sex, the noise from them loud and thumping, someone's voice yowling, the other voice grunting. It felt like the whole house was in on it. She hurriedly finished and ran out before they reached the end. On the way home, she nearly had an orgasm at a red light, so aroused was she by Troy and how she imagined he was going at it in the next room. That she'd overheard them infuriated her. She couldn't recall instructions on how to deal with this sort of thing in her professional guidelines.

The atmosphere in the Jordan house that evening affected Poppy, who, sensing something wrong, fussed and was unhappy. Both parents gave themselves over to her, distracting themselves with her care. Long after the little girl went to sleep, Hallie and Troy were still knocking about the first floor, tidying up as though cleanliness might save them. Unable to stand being awake any longer they finally went to bed.

Anger came in waves for Hallie. She worried about Poppy. The older kids would take care of their sister as everyone aged, as she and Troy passed on, but that wasn't what flayed at her. It was her child's immutable innocence. Like light, this moving, diapered light. Hallie responded with such a need to protect her that a threat of any kind sent her soul raging against the universe, screaming at it from inside her head.

Troy was awake. She thought he might be crying. Like a lover bereft. She remembered him before the theft, anticipating his company's future, a new machine for the newly designed bags, ecologically sound, his war against plastic. For months, so much excitement and wonder. Like a teenager with a first love. He was heartbroken.

What would they do?

Her job was suddenly important. Teaching remedial math had flattered her sense of civic spirit, the extra cash allowing her to hire someone to fix that worthless sort of room off the kitchen. She'd teach more classes. But that would leave her less time for Poppy. She'd need more time for the child now that she couldn't pay for Poppy's team. Only she'd have to work more hours—

They'd sell the place, of course. Pay off the mortgage. Maybe sell it themselves to save on the agent's fee. Yes. They'd do that. They'd have everyone they knew over, a goodbye party and—Does anyone know anyone looking to buy a house? A sell-the-house party. Her spirits rose at the idea of everyone coming inside to them, one last time. Soon, she thought, before it's all over.

The following morning, Cecile let herself into the Jordan house. She was wearing her best clothes, expecting a group of people to see the tented room reveal. Instead, she was alone. She waited. She took photographs. When she felt she'd captured every angle, she waited some more. Hallie finally came downstairs and into the kitchen, a mean, bitter expression on her face. Poppy was walking with her, holding her hand.

Cecile said, "Ready when you are!"

Hallie let the little girl go in first and followed. "Oh. Very nice. Yeah." She laughed. "My God. It's actually magnificent." She leaned against the doorway. "Oh my God," she said as though completely defeated. "I'm going to have to. I knew I would." Cecile was amazed at the woman's response. Poppy turned and toddled out of the room. Hallie followed the girl. "Poppy. Come with Mommy."

And wouldn't you know, Cecile thought, catching some errant threads. At eye level beside the doorjamb. She used her thumbnail to tuck them under the fabric. She searched around in case there were more. Sure enough, at the angle where the baseboard met the molding.

On her knees doing a quick fix, she heard a car move along the driveway. She wondered if Troy had come home again in the middle of the day. Back on her feet, her face close to the edge surrounding the door, she gave it a last going over.

"Honestly," she laughed, thinking Hallie was still close. "Two tiny threads. There's always something, isn't there."

No response came. She went out to the kitchen. Hallie and Poppy had disappeared. She called out. No one answered.

Hallie's number was on her cell, and when she tried it, she heard it ringing on the second floor. Calling Hallie's name again, she walked through the house. She found the door that led to the basement and hollered down. Nothing.

Angry now, she decided to stay until someone appeared. All day if she had to. The final bill was in an envelope in her purse. She went into the living room and sat where she could see most of the first floor. No one would get by her. After about twenty minutes, she heard a car again. It was Hallie driving up with Poppy.

"God," Hallie said on her way in. "I can't get my head around anything." Settling the child in her left arm to free her right hand, she began pulling cash from her purse. The money, with the distinctive blue line announcing these were hundred dollar bills, was folded and jammed into Cecile's hand. "Grab it while it's going," she said, her eyes tearing. "No more where that came from."

Cecile felt it would be bad form to count it out. She closed her bandaged fingers around all the cash. It had an unanticipated feel. She had expected a check.

Hallie went into the tented room with Poppy. Her voice harsh, she told Cecile, "I was right. It does make the rest of the house look like crap."

"I could do the living room if—"

"No, no. God no. We're selling the place."

"What?"

"I'm having everyone over for a party. The last stand at the Jordans'."

We need to unload it, like yesterday." She stared at the walls and ceiling of the room, and her face began to soften. "Yeah. I'll miss this. It's so beautiful. Beautiful."

Cecile felt her breath getting shallow. New owners might not like a tented room. What if they tore it out? "Why?"

"So we can start over. You should buy it. Do you want it? The roof has to be replaced, and the furnace gets wonky."

Unsure of what to say—a simple no seemed rude—Cecile asked, "How much do you want for it?"

"Whatever. As much as we can get." She put her hand over the back of Poppy's hair, stroking it. "And we'll have a big party. This was a good house. We're having a big send-off. Goodbye house. We have a lot of friends. Someone might know someone. Otherwise, I call a realtor. Whatever."

Cecile said carefully, "Can I help you set up? For the party? I can do up a table so it's—"

"No! This is crackers and a bowl of punch. They won't be coming for the food."

"I won't charge. I mean, I'll just do it for free, like an ad for myself."

"Oh." Hallie said. She seemed to bring Cecile into focus. "Okay. If you want to." Taking another look at the room, she said, "You should come to the party. Right? You have to be here. People will ask how you did this. I couldn't tell them. Come, okay?"

It was after five, and Rodge made himself a drink.

"I'm so late," Cecile cried as she hurried in. The amount of worry in her voice alarmed him. "I don't want to be early to this thing, but I don't want to be too late either."

"Are these clowns some kind of royalty?"

"You aren't drinking are you!"

"No."

"Where's your good jacket?"

The way she was fluttering all over made him want to catch her as though she were a huge bird let loose in the place. She yelped when he got his hands on her. When he began roving down her breasts, she yelped louder and hurried away. The bathroom door was slammed in his face. He heard the shower running. Furious, he had another drink.

And another quick one before he took his own shower and, later, because the idea of her excitement about the rich people was really annoying him, a very short one before letting Cecile help him into the new jacket she'd bought him. His old jackets no longer buttoned across the front. When he thought she wasn't looking, he threw back one more before they left. "Honey," she said in a strong voice. "You don't need that."

As he drove, she held on to the handle above her window.

"Where is this place," he asked in a voice that told her the place couldn't be anywhere good.

"You'll like them."

He said nothing.

"And I have to tell you, my God, she wasn't kidding about cheap food," Cecile laughed. He recognized her bright and cheery come-on-Rodge voice. "Wait'll you see. Saltines. A block of cheddar. And this punch bowl. I helped her get this silver monstrosity out of the attic. A couple of cans of fruit juice and a gallon of cheap gin. Otherwise there's a pitcher of tap water. I'm still laughing. It's that she just didn't care. She thought the whole thing a big hoot. But I arranged it so it really looks, just, oh my God. And all I did was take some leaves from a catalpa tree I found near the back of the garage and some sprigs of euonymus. I think she appreciated what I did. The table looked incredible. It's good to be friends with people. The punch bowl belonged to her great grandmother. It took me over an hour to polish it. And right next to it, she sticks this tower of plastic party cups. I'm serious. Those little—"

"All *right*."

"All right, what?" She waited.

He was silent.

"Rodge, just be yourself. They'll love you. Just the way you are is fine."

His hands tightened on the steering wheel.

They had to drive three blocks beyond the address to find a parking spot.

At the front door, he sucked his gut in hard. Affecting a very formal tone, he said, "Now. My dear." He held the door open. "After you."

Gently, she said, "You might stick to water."

A lot of noise. There was a crowd of people.

"Everyone!" Rodge said in a loud greeting, his hand up.

The people closest turned, smiled, made room.

She went into the dining room and almost hollered. The catalpa leaves and euonymus sprigs were piled up like compost behind the plate of crackers. The rest of her greens, as she looked, were on the floor. The table was covered with unmatched platters of deviled eggs, meatballs stuck with toothpicks, rolled ham slices, bite-size quiches, cookies. Of course, Hallie's friends. But didn't Hallie know her friends would bring food? Without thinking, Cecile moved a few sprigs and leaves, freeing them and then rearranging them. She heard, "Excuse me," and moved to let a woman who'd entered the house behind her with a dish of crudités and dip find some space. Cecile introduced herself while stifling a little rage. Stay on course. Meet everyone. The table design was a freebie. The first people into the house would've noticed it, and that's more than enough.

She turned to Rodge, wanting to encourage him to eat something, but he was pouring out two glasses of punch, and she took one from him, thanking him.

"By all means," he said, "my dear."

"What?"

"Should I make a toast to you," he said, smiling.

It was then that she heard Hallie's voice from the kitchen saying, "That's her." She looked over. Hallie and a few women were grinning at her as she called, "Cecile!"

The woman beside Hallie yelled, "That room!"

Cecile realized others had turned to see who she was.

"Come see it," Cecile said to Rodge.

As she moved to join Hallie, she realized Rodge had noticed the greeting she'd been given. And she saw from the corner of her eye that he didn't like it. He picked up the ladle and replenished the punch in his cup, his expression full of injury.

She threaded her way through the crowd to get to the kitchen. Here she began to realize the people around the Jordans were the same hodgepodge as the furniture, unmatched and plain or beautiful or young or very old. Her spirits lifted; the mix augured a place for her too. And weren't they all talking with such animation! The party went at a faster speed than any party she'd been to before. She stepped with buoyancy into the kitchen. To let her pass, a number of arms lifted cups containing the juice-colored gin of the punch, and this put her in mind of weddings where the bride steps under a salute of swords.

"Oh," she laughed, ducking to get through. She felt very young. She joined Hallie and her friends at the doorway of the tented room. The lights from the hanging fixture and the sconces she'd installed had the place looking magical.

"You did this?" One of Hallie's friends asked her. "How did you do this!"

"You like?" Cecile laughed. Yes, she happened to have some of her cards with her. "No job too small," she sang out softly. "And the bigger the better. Anything and everything." She remained near the decorated room while this group lauded her. Her heart filled. Were her feet even touching the floor? If I can't make something beautiful, she thought, I don't want to live.

Rodge supposed he should squeeze into the kitchen and see the room, but instead, he lifted his chin in a signal to Cecile. She should follow him. He was going into the living room. That's where it seemed obvious party guests should go. They didn't belong in the back of some kitchen.

Two couples standing near the sofa were deep in conversation. He moved near them, stumbling slightly over the rug.

One of the men said, "I don't think four hundred. Maybe three fifty?" They were pricing the house, he realized. He moved a little closer. The talk turned to mortgages and interest rates.

Rodge said, "Hah," and the four people turned, smiling at him.

"How much would you say they'd get?" one of them asked.

"I wouldn't buy a whole house," Rodge said. The words felt sticky on their way out of his mouth. "I'm in . . . condo. Gotta condo. Right." They stared at him. Then they turned away.

He went back to the dining room. To a young woman nearby, he said, "Looks like the well might rush dry."

She gave a cursory look into the punch bowl before moving past him.

As he drank from his refilled cup, he caught sight of Cecile in the kitchen. Her head was thrown back, her mouth wide open. Her eyes were closed. She was crying out, "Oh!" and the group around her was laughing.

He went back into the living room and kept going. He ended up in the hallway. The hallway was covered with family photos. He went over and looked at them. Bending close, he wanted evidence of privilege. Cecile should see this, he thought. Vacation pictures of people who hadn't paid her. That cash she'd come home with hadn't fooled him. He believed the wads of bills had come from her own savings account to save her pride, to convince him the Jordans weren't stringing her along. Meanwhile, she was over here polishing their silver all afternoon for nothing. He had to save her from this mess she'd gotten herself into.

He didn't hear Troy descending the staircase.

Troy had put Poppy to bed. The idea of the party had seemed crazy enough to him to wrestle his feelings onto a mat, pinning them down and leaving him agog. Distraction was carrying him for the moment. That was the immediate plan. He was halfway down the stairs when he spotted the comb-over and the enormous gut on a middle-aged stranger. The man was inspecting each of the family photos with a pronounced sneer on his face. The sneer was aimed at pictures of the older two, Troy's son and daughter. Babies and then toddlers, his children maturing through beach trips and graduation pictures. And then Hallie with the newborn, and from Hallie's arm, a waterfall of blankets all the way to her sandals and, peeping from the crook of her arm, a pink knitted cap. Whoever this man was, he gave a snort before draining his cup, after which he turned to walk back through the house.

In the dining room, Rodge picked up the ladle in the punch bowl. He saw Cecile spot him from the far end of the kitchen. She shot her hand up. He glared at her. Her face, and her hand flapping, told him to come and look. Her expression promised it was fun. His glare replied all this nonsense had gone on long enough. Two men beside her joined in. Now he had a trio waving him forward. They looked like cartoons. He turned his attention to the punch, scraping up the last of it.

Troy had followed him. "Who are you?"

Rodge smiled at his host. "I'm Rodge," he told Troy and put down the ladle. He held out his hand. "Cecile's husband."

Troy ignored his hand. "Rodge Collette? You're an interior decorator too?"

"Debrett. I'm Rodge *Debrett*. And I work at University *Hospital*."

"What are you, a doctor?"

"A doctor? No. Not exactly." He pulled at the edge of his new jacket with the hand that had been refused.

"What are you?"

Rodge took his time, wanting to frame a title for himself that might flatten this son of a bitch. "You think I'm one of the docs? No, your error." He felt his balance go off kilter and grabbed the side of the table. As he steadied himself, he had a glancing view of his wife and the women and men around her watching him with alarm. Watch this, he wanted to tell them. "Listen," he said. "A doc? I'm the man who makes sure those doctors get paid." His heart seized a bit just then because he believed the other man was about to hit him. He braced his feet on the floor, fists up, ready to return a punch.

Troy didn't hit him. He turned his back on him and walked away.

Rodge hollered, "What am I? You want to know what I am?" and unzipped his fly.

Cecile saw this and so did the people around her. A few more heads turned in his direction and, with that, more and more people turning to see what had everyone suddenly paralyzed. His hand pulled out his wrinkled, fleshy *coup du ciel* as Cecile had happily named it. It moved, growing slightly as though sensing many people. Turning its singular eye, *Who all is here in anticipation?* Then the thick hand of its owner directed it down. Rodge peed into his cup, a few drops ricocheting up, the noise echoing in the sudden silence. He poured the cup into the punch bowl, a torrential noise given the hush. To the sound of his wife crying out to him, he did this a second time for good measure.

The house with the tented room sold quickly. The furniture was sold, too, and one of the cars. Until a plan was in place, the Jordans moved in with Hallie's mother, who lived in a bungalow in Bay Village with her partner and her partner's dog, a Great Pyrenees. The dog, a natural nanny, hovered over Poppy, who grabbed its fur and hugged it, followed it, fed it, and often napped against its heavy belly.

The two elder Jordan children came home to find work and cheap rooms. They were there at dinner when Hallie's sisters and brother came over with their partners. The dining room was crowded. A chair had to be brought in from the garage. Hallie now and then put her hand on Troy's back, rubbing the soft fabric of his shirt. It was less support for Troy—though it was that—than a warning to the others not to pile on with advice or opinions. The two grown children watched their father as though unable to recognize him. When Troy announced he'd begin again and it would be even better, it was a non sequitur. Hallie's mother brought up the affection the dog had for Poppy. She told anecdotes about previous family dogs, devious terriers and foolish hounds, but the stories gained only a little flight before losing air.

Finally someone asked, "Who was that guy? At the party?"

The room came to life. Hallie and Troy began laughing.

"Oh my God, that guy!"

"I will never drink gin again in my life."

"Or punch. Nothing liquid."

"But who *was* he?"

"That's what he was saying. That guy. He was telling Troy who he was."

"I didn't care who he was."

"He came in with Hallie's decorator."

"Did she bill you for it?"

"He was the only thing that made me glad to sell the house. I couldn't eat in that dining room again."

As they laughed, talking about the party, Hallie looked for the dog. There. Once she found the dog, she saw Poppy, her lifeline, an antidote. Seeing Poppy, she felt her breath come deep and steady. She sat back, calm now, and felt her son's arm around her. She heard her grown daughter's voice, "You should go into catering, Mom."

"Beatrix Windsor," Cecile, now Beatrix, introduced herself to the woman. They'd left St. Paul's after Mass at about the same time, and the woman looked approachable. "I'm new to Grosse Pointe, to Michigan in fact."

"Oh. Welcome. You'll like it here."

"Just hoping to find things peaceful."

"This isn't a business move?"

She turned for a quick look at the lake before they headed into the parking lot. "I lost my husband." She didn't mention how.

"Oh, I'm so sorry. I shouldn't have asked."

"I wanted to kind of start fresh. Away from memories."

"I don't blame you."

"And my business is portable. I'm an interior decorator."

"A decorator."

She would not be downhearted. The divorce had left her nearly penniless, but enough remained after they sold the condo to cover an apartment rental and new business cards. She found part-time book-keeping work, something to hold her until Beatrix Windsor Interiors began taking on clients. Her ads were already in the bulletins of her new churches. She had not been afraid to knock on doors of design shops and show photos of the tented room. One owner said she might be used, as he'd put it, for any overflow. Just that slight promise had thrilled her. To keep her spirits high, she worked evenings on her living room. Her landlady was impressed. And the landlady might know people.

There were nights she was tempted to go back to a dating sight and find another man. A fantasy of romantic moments tempted her. There were times she longed for the bustle of children, of pets and schedules and hurrying, the measure a shared life would take of her. But then she'd sketch out a solution to the problem of a room and become so engaged she'd question if love was really in her best interest. People didn't blossom beneath her talents the way a sofa or a wall could. Burned bridges and a foolish man be damned, she could be happy. Michigan would get beautiful. She had her passion.

The Expert

ON CABLE NEWS just now, here's the face of Derek Cowper. An expert on something. His hair was gone.

"Huh," I said. "Hello Derek. It's been years."

"You know him?"

"I went out with him."

"You did not."

"On a date. I was twenty-two."

"He's a billionaire."

"Is he?"

"Where did he take you?"

"To dinner."

"You could've been Derek Cowper's wife!"

"Right. I was *this* close."

"Mrs. Derek Cowper! How did you meet him?"

By looking up from a file. Here he comes toward my section of the office in a coffee-colored suit. "I've been assigned to your desk," he'd said.

I would have cut him enormous slack. No one just came into that room. If you did, you'd feel like an alien. Now and then, a sales rep came by or someone from senior management, but we were like most inner organs of large companies, encyclopedic and dismissive. The section was called Specialty Desks and took up a corner of the fifth floor: rate calculations, group reservations, complaints, and—where I sat—prepaid tickets.

"We're hiring?" I asked him. "I wasn't told I'd be training someone."

He told me the name of the management consulting firm he worked for.

Oh, I thought, that's who he is.

The latest CEO of our airline had hired an outside contractor to improve us. There was a recession on, the price of fuel had gone up, and the industry had been deregulated. We were losing money, and before our stockholders sold out, they might be impressed by the efforts of men like Derek Cowper, who were paid to ride in and teach us efficiency.

He found a chair and got out a leather bound pad and a pencil. "Describe what you do."

"Okay. A guy walks into a travel agency. He wants to pay for someone overseas to come visit—a relative from Zagreb or Belgrade or servicemen's wives from Vietnam. Unaccompanied children from Beirut. You kind of get a picture of the world when you notice who's—"

"No. I don't need that. I need how you process it."

"Right. First thing I do is call the bank for the day's currency conversion. Then I calculate the fare. The agent collects the money. I wire the ticket order to our station overseas with the passenger's name and contact. Then I flag dates on the calendar to make sure the flight is booked, the agent gets the arrival information, and I send an alert to the airport staff if this person needs help. If they can't speak English."

Cowper wrote all of what I said in longhand.

I waited.

When he came to the end of my last sentence, he closed the notebook, put the pencil in its holder, and, leaning forward, began reading the file names in the bin beside my desk. "If you could streamline your efforts what would you do?"

"I've already done it," I said and pulled up one of the files. "See? I don't log everything in, I staple everything as it happens. One on top of the other. You can read the progress. It saves a whole lot of time not having to write everything out."

He had his leather notebook open again and wrote all this down. Turning the pencil over, he erased "stable," brushed the rubber dust from the page with the edge of his hand, and, righting the pencil, wrote "staple." Then he bent forward, reading closely the open file's dispatches. "How come a passenger from Saigon is ticketed from Bangkok?"

"It's cheaper," I told him. "Bangkok to Los Angeles is half the price of Saigon to LA. The Saigon office pulls the Bangkok to Saigon coupon and throws it away because here's the passenger right there, ready to board. The prepayer is a serviceman bringing his wife here. The fare is hiked up because it's a war zone. This way, he only pays half."

"Isn't that illegal?"

"Why would it be illegal?"

"He isn't paying the full rate."

"But he is if the passenger left from Bangkok. That's farther."

"But the passenger's not leaving from Bangkok."

"I'm sure it's not illegal. Don't put illegal down."

He went on to other questions and continued to write out what I told him for about an hour and then left.

That was the last I thought I'd see of him. The next day, late in the afternoon, he came back to my desk and asked me if I'd like to go out to dinner with him. He said he'd made a study of New York. I was going to be surprised at how well he could pick a place to eat.

"You know, I grew up here," I told him.

"All the better."

"You're on."

I met him after work in the lobby. We hurried through the revolving doors and walked, canted forward in a stiff wind up Park Avenue. The wind was blowing dirt around us. I had the habit of saying yes to anyone offering a free dinner, a supplement to my low pay, and as we walked, I realized I was already eating tiny particles of the city.

He was telling me about businesses he had, one of them to do with selling key rings and pens to college bookstores. "Colleges are killers," he said. "They keep my margins at only twenty-seven percent."

I wasn't sure what this meant.

He told me the administrations were screwing him. "They work up their brands and then keep a total monopoly. I'm doing them a service putting their logo on a keychain." Something about licensing. "Really grinds me," he said. But he didn't seem ground. He seemed energized, like a fighter on his way to the ring.

Twenty blocks later, he found our destination, "That didn't take so long," he said. "I don't know why people bother with cabs."

I'm not sure if I ever got the name of the place. There were a lot of those bars uptown, narrow, with asymmetrical lighting and exotic-looking wood. "Have some," he yelled over the noise. It was happy hour, packed with men making a sea of navy blue worsted and women skilled at draping a coat over the back of a chair so the designer label was visible.

Derek led the way to a long, narrow table covered with hors d'oeuvres: stuffed mushrooms, roasted pecans, bruschetta. All free. This wasn't unusual, though the variety was. The mushrooms were stuffed with herbed bread, and I realized they increased my thirst. Derek was popping food into his mouth as though a gentle motor was attached to his elbow, a quick adjustment agreed upon by his fingers as mushroom to nut to bread slice was picked up, raised, and popped in.

Food was an easy freebie because the bars made so much from selling drinks, though I never knew what they charged for—say, wine, that night—because he asked for two glasses of water.

Handing one to me, he had to yell again to be heard over the noise, "I can guess you never knew this place existed."

"Hah," I said, but his attention had turned to the cherry tomatoes.

After he'd depleted the smorgasbord and we finished the water, he led me through the crush of bodies and out into the street. "You should have had the quails' eggs," he said. "That was the protein."

We walked west for a few blocks until we were looking across Fifth Avenue at Central Park. I think he mentioned the zoo.

"I'm going to have to have dinner," I told him.

His hand was on his stomach as though he'd eaten too much. "You want to go all the way back to the bar?" He checked his watch. "I'm not sure the food will still be out."

"No. I want to find a restaurant."

It was as though I'd asked him to run into the zoo and bring me back a penguin; he wasn't sure it was necessary, let alone possible. Arms out, he looked up and down the avenue until he spotted a food cart. It was three blocks down. He hurried toward it. I followed. He ordered a hot dog.

"Everything on it," he said with a kind of abandon.

Everything to put on it was free. Also there would have been no admission charge for the zoo. He pulled out a small leather change purse from which his fingers squeezed out quarters and a nickel and then some dimes.

"I can pay for it," I told him.

"It's already done," he said. Indeed, he found the final nickel and two pennies.

After I'd eaten some of the hot dog—he didn't want any—I asked him, "Are you going to make your life's work management consulting?"

He laughed. "I have other plans." From a pocket, he pulled out a small case. "This is what I meant to do when I was in your office. But they moved me to a different floor after I gave them my suggestions for your desk."

"What suggestions? *You* had suggestions?"

"Here," he said as he slipped business cards from the case and handed them to me. "If you would pass these around, maybe figure the best person to give one to."

The cards said, "Derek Cowper Promotions." There was a New York phone number.

"Is this your college bookstore business?"

"No, this is promotion work."

"Promoting what?"

"Anything. Anything and everything. Is six enough? I only want a few people in each office to get one. That'll make it look exclusive."

"You mean give them to my friends?"

"Your coworkers. You would know which person might know someone. People with connections. That's who we want to get on board."

After I finished the hot dog, he walked me to a subway entrance, and I went home.

"Did you kiss him good-night?"

"No, I did not kiss him good-night."

"Do you still have the cards?"

"No, of course not."

"So you gave them out? His cards!"

"No, I did not give out his cards."

"Is he, like, a lot older than you?"

"I think we're about the same age."

"How come you're not as rich? What were you doing with your time?"

"I had some plans."

"You could've learned his game, passed him by, let him eat your dust."

Cowper was offering advice on CNN. Foreign policy.

"I decided to travel. There was a flight to Sweden. I jumped on board. In Malmö, I met your grandfather. We took the long way home. That's why your mother was born in India."

"That's just—what were you even doing?"

What was I ever doing? Those years of short skirts and high heels, a first apartment, new friends, the city at night. "I was young," I said. "It was like I owned the whole world."

"You could've been rich."

On CNN, Derek's left hand was visible as he drove home his point on how to manage the world's economy. I could see his wedding band. The sympathy we women can extend to each other can come so quickly and deeply.

Adam

WHEN THE WHALE song of the elevator reached him on the seventeenth floor, Adam put down the garbage bag holding his clothes, redid his grip on it, and heaved it again up and over his shoulder in time to step into the car as the doors opened.

In the lobby, a few of his dorm-mates were going out ahead of him. Korean and some Chinese and then the three guys from Cambodia. The building housed only a few Anglos, the term he liked for himself, though he was a quarter Nicaraguan. One quarter from the Nicaraguan side. Also, one quarter Anglo. He was on his way to meet his father, who would supply him with the other half of his gene pool—the mystery. Another Anglo? He liked the term. It sounded like *gringo* and made him see himself with a black eye patch, riding a spotted horse through the sagebrush, a knife in his teeth, and greenbacks in his saddlebag.

Curving walks brought Adam through the campus, walks lined with evergreen bushes and leading to the older buildings near the main gates. By the time he reached the sidewalk and the avenue in front of the school, he was sweating. He found a sunny spot near the curb and placed the garbage bag beside his foot. On time. He checked again. Right on time for his dad.

Dad.

He began imagining Ben Quilt, his father, and replayed in his head the man's guarded voice. Curt but not unfriendly. That voice, the first time he heard it, sure he'd found the right man, slid about his insides like a loose razor blade. Placing his father inside a frat house as a young man or seeing him in a later rendition, running a business, Adam practiced in his head the ways he'd put the man at ease. His dad was a shy man; witness the lack of information online for any person named Benjamin Quilt. He'd Googled. Up came pages about bedspreads.

He'd act very chill. But a pool and a pool table—items of this sort would make conversation so much easier. Surely the reason his father hadn't tied himself down with Adam's mother was to live large. Adam could kid his dad about his possessions but in a fun way, make him feel things were all right with Adam. No accusations would be forthcoming. No complaints. And absolutely *no rage*. Just, Okay, here we are. Relax, Dad, *I am not angry*.

He took a deep breath of the wintery air. Almost time. He rocked very slightly forward and back. Checking the time again, he brought up his phone and then put it back in his pocket. Almost but not quite five.

"Sure," a very casual "sure," his father had said when Adam reached him by phone. A second "sure" when he agreed to the pickup place. "Five."

Terse, spare with his words, like the best lawmen. The good poker player kind of man. The idea that his father's work might be financial schemes took Adam's fancy, and he kept an eye out for a sleek Ferrari or something equal. Only a few moments into this reverie, and he worried his father might take him for a con artist out to grab inheritance. Were there more Quilt men (or women for that matter), stepbrothers and sisters who wouldn't like someone else coming in on the family money? He thought of recording on his phone an idea for a movie about step-children attacking the brilliant young man who's arrived to save their father. He left the phone in his pocket. It was getting dark, and his dad might see only someone on his phone, no one else, and drive away.

A car steamed unsteadily up the road before drifting rightward to-ward the curb, a bulbous white Dodge, freckled with rust, the visor down over the driver's side of the windshield, like the very eye patch an Anglo might like. It slid closer and came to rest in front of him. Adam stared at it a moment, unsure whether to wave the guy on. He saw the driver lean across the passenger seat. The passenger door flew open with an animal scream. Adam moved forward and looked into the car. A large arm in a cut-off sweatshirt was visible with a tattoo very faded and weedy with long, gray hairs. The owner of the arm was looking up at him. When Adam got a good look at his face, it was Adam himself he saw. His face looked back at him transformed—not so much older as beaten up, a let-this-be-a-lesson-to-you face.

"Get in," the man said.

Adam gathered up the garbage bag in both arms and climbed in, sitting forward so his backpack had room. When he turned toward the driver, he noticed deep acne scars and mottled skin, smelled kitchen grease, and heard the man huffing with labored breath. Adam offered him a head-nodding, shoulder-shaking "Hey!" Then he looked down at his feet. Bending forward, he released the heel of his left desert boot where it was caught. Rust had worn a hole on the passenger side floor. He could see the street. With this in mind, he arranged his bag so it was comfortable on his lap, planting his feet on either side of the hole. "So. All right. So, hey."

"Shut the door."

"Oh." Adam turned to find the bottom of his door stuck in the soft earth. He leaned far out to grasp the handle and heft it up. He then yanked it forward. It screamed slowly as he brought it over the curb and almost to the car. On his second try, he pulled hard enough to close it.

"Awesome," Adam said. "So. Hi."

"Yeah," his father said, his eye on his side-view mirror. He brought the car shuddering slowly into traffic.

They drove along Main Street. The car had no shocks and rocked like a baby carriage. There were storefronts opposite the campus, bars, and lunch places. As they passed L'Americain Café and All Day Breakfast, Ben said, "That's where I work."

"Yeah?" Adam kept his face forward. He'd become uncomfortable. Unable to look directly at the man's face, he glanced down the faded and splotchy blue jeans that covered the man's right leg until his eye caught on an enormous and very bright white sneaker resting against the accelerator. Visible, sticking up from the top eyelet, was the plastic loop that would have held a price tag.

"I'm their chef. So. That's the paycheck."

A few moments passed. Adam asked, "So, like, you make omelets?"

"Yeah."

"Waffles? Like that?"

"Yeah."

"Awesome."

At the far end of the city, the stores gave way to off-campus housing. They passed a large corner house the color of strawberries. A group of students stood on the lawn around a small grill with a fire. He wanted one of them to see him, to come running to his rescue and, almost simultaneously, wanted never to be noticed in this car by anyone.

The college housing receded, and there was a stretch of woods and some train tracks. They drove until a break from this view opened on a field dusted with light snow, beyond which was a freshly painted farmhouse near a barn of extensive length, the cooling fans on the end of the barn not unlike the bladed circles of jet engines.

"That's an egg farm," Ben told him. "I worked in there once."

Adam looked over at the white clapboard building, which didn't look like anything except for the huge fans on the end. He wanted to pull out his phone and record an idea for how the engines might start and take the barn into a road race.

His father said, "So I know which came first. It was the chicken."

"I thought you lived in West Grove."

"I did. With a friend. That's over."

They drove for another fifteen minutes and reached Harbinger and its medical center and its many antique shops, another set of tracks, and as they made a turn north at the center of town, they passed the storefront and marquee, posters and a box office sign. Adam realized his father hadn't noticed the place.

"That's Harbinger Theater. I was in a play there. *Hamlet.*"

The older man was silent for a while. "Think I missed that one. *Hamlet.*"

"Not a bad play. Nothing happens till the end, though."

"Long as it gets there."

Adam released one hand from the garbage bag and felt around his chest, afraid his heart might be misfiring.

They drove down a hill and into a neighborhood of one- and two-story houses, a few of which were boarded up, though the ones not boarded up looked empty. They took a left along a street that seemed bucolic, with empty lots, with hills and small valleys backed by evergreens. Another turn where they drove to the end of the block. There, in the crescent of a copse of trees was a red-shingled house whose naked windows stared back at them. Ben drove up the driveway, the car dipping heavily forward as the brakes were applied.

"This is it," Ben said and tilted his head. "Home sweet home."

"You live here?"

"Since Monday. It's a little on the raw side, I'll be the first to admit. But that was the deal." Ben stepped out, stretching, displaying a heavy gut.

Adam sat, mesmerized by the sight of the house and, nearby, the sight of this man, his father. In the features of the face, there was no mistaking the resemblance of father to son. Adam had studied his own face looking for this man, since nothing in his mother's Nicaraguan features resembled his own. And now, here he was. He watched as his father bent toward him.

"You gonna sit there all day?"

Adam struggled with the door and the bag. When he was standing close to the house, he followed Ben's glance to the roof where part of the gutter had come loose. The free end was bent and pointed toward the ground.

"A few nails. See what I'm saying? A few shingles. Then I'm in. A homeowner."

Adam followed him through a side door and up three steps into a dark kitchen. A small refrigerator and stove sat out from the wall; broken plaster and lathe remained where there had been cabinets.

Ben said, "Make yourself at home."

Adam stood with his arms around his bag of clothing. He was looking at an electric outlet that was half off the wall and poised like a diver. Reaching over, he pressed it back to the wall, but it bounced back out when he let go.

"One more thing to take care of, I guess." Ben said. He seemed poised himself between making a joke of the house and threatening anyone who criticized it. "Yeah, whoever left it like this was royally pissed off is what I think. It's kind of . . . you can see for yourself. All potential. It's the potential you always got to look out for. Not what's really here. Potential is the whole game. I bring this place up to code in four months, and I get to stay."

"This is, like, you bought this?"

"Sort of. I'm kind of applying to be the buyer. I got four months to fix it."

"I see. I see." Adam was looking up at the ceiling, which gave way near the center, the gray square tiles like a torn skirt. From under the tiles, three wires twirled down to a bare light bulb. He took a deep breath. The garbage bag began to weigh in his arms.

"I get a day off every week," Ben said. "That's when I'll turn this place around. You know what they say. If the place is yours, you work ten times as hard."

Over the dining room walls, there remained a wallpaper of dim green sectioned by trellises with ivy and an occasional blue flower. A small chandelier of iron in the shape of a wagon wheel hung above a card table. Around the table were three chairs.

Ben flicked the light switch on, but the room remained dark. "Don't know what the problem is there." He tried the switch again. "Not cooperating."

There was enough natural light for the two men to make their way. The living room fireplace was intact. Some loose twigs and leaves were in the hearth. On the mantel were papers.

Adam peered over at them. "Red Sled." He picked them up to read. "Red Sled Realty, LLC."

"That's my guys," his father said.

"Good brand," Adam told him.

"You know them?"

"Never heard of them. My business professor's always saying how important your name is. Red Sled is a name you'd remember. It rhymes. They got a big sled flying over chimneys. See, there's a big bag with little houses on the sled. Like they're gifts. So you think of Christmas."

"Trust me, they ain't Santa Claus," Ben said.

"They're a subsidiary."

"You know that?"

"It's what it says. It's for the holding company to do real estate in Michigan. If I started a business, I'd do layups on the Quilt name. Quilt is my brand. My mom put your name on my birth certificate. She's like that . . . everything *official*. Otherwise, I might not have found you."

Embarrassment followed this remark, and they turned back to their inspection of the place.

About the table in the dining room, "You could have poker games," Adam said, nodding his head toward the other room. He began walking around, the garbage bag now like a child growing restless. He pointed to the faded plaid sofa, listing to one side beneath the front windows. "You could do whatever you wanted, no one telling you. Watch TV in the middle of the day with the volume up loud." He grinned at his father and the man's eyes took on a helpless, pleading look.

They moved to the staircase, Ben testing the newel for the depth of wobble. "Not too bad," he said.

Adam followed Ben up the stairs. Both men were used to hearing stair treads give and even groan beneath their weight. Adam took note of his father's gray hair curling against the etched lines in his neck, the neck adorned with black moles, red freckles, pockmarks and eraser-sized bumps; the gray sweatshirt that hung loose on his back; the flat khaki pants, worn pale and shiny over the seat; and, cushioning his every step, the enormous pair of bright-white sneakers.

Adam was overwhelmed with confusion. It was his mother who'd always told him to adjust to what life threw at you. *Whatever house you walk into, you always act nice, never be impressed and never look down on anyone. Ever.* He was trying to do this. Not a very neat or tidy kid, the tour of the house held something of an adventure. He'd felt too constricted growing up. Bullied, excluded, and dateless. That he had a father at all was almost too much to believe.

The upstairs hallway seemed intact. Adam nodded his head as he looked around. They walked into a large bedroom at the front of the house, where a wide, unmade mattress had been set against the far wall and a pile of clothes lay on the floor.

"Getting moved in," Ben murmured.

They walked to a smaller front bedroom.

"Got your own room," he said.

And Adam said, "Awesome."

A futon was in the middle of the room, covered with a fitted sheet that had horses printed on it. The last, and very small, bedroom was empty.

Adam went into the bathroom and reared backward at the smell, the dark water and rust stains, the pitted tub.

Ben said, "Yeah. I gotta bring the plumbing up to code, too, so we just work with what we got for a while."

After Adam dumped his bag and backpack in his room, he took out his laptop and followed his father back downstairs.

"So now you got the tour," Ben said. "No charge for tours. So. What do you need . . . do you need anything?"

"You got any beer?"

"Yeah. I got beer. I got some chips too."

"You got chips!"

"Yeah."

"You got chips!"

"I got beer in a cooler. I keep chips in the refrigerator because the ants."

"Whoa, chips! Beer! Contraband!"

Adam, taking a can of beer from Ben and a big bag of tortilla chips, went back out to the living room and sat heavily down on the sofa. He popped the top carefully and took a long draft. From the bag, he drew out a large triangle and held it in front of his face.

"Verboten," he said before stuffing the tortilla chip into his mouth. "Mmmm." He took up the can of beer and emptied much of it into his mouth. He sat back. "Ahh. This is the life."

"Yeah. This is how I do it." Ben said. He sat on the higher end of the sofa.

"I have to live in the bat cave," Adam said. "Great-granny's house. It's like a hundred stories high with some of the gingerbread falling off, and all the rooms are dark, and she and my gramma's always after me to get on some ladder and fix something. And there's, like," he began laughing, "radar on you every second, like it's nuclear-powered GPS, so they always know where you are. Like, they know what you think, too, and before you even think it. You would hate that house. Any man around it is free labor."

His thumb dusted off salt from his fingertips. "And Gramma's like, 'We don't want a mistake. We don't need any more mistakes.' Like we don't know who she's talking about. Boo pee doo. My mom says to just humor her because she had to leave the convent. Gramma was in Nicaragua being a missionary and was left behind in a building. It got surrounded by soldiers. Whatever side they were, when the rest of the nuns got back, they found her, and then they made her leave the convent and go home. I found out it's because she was having my mom. And she, like, never talks to my mom. You should see. If they're in the same room? She won't even look at my mom. So I'm up on the ladder fixin' the gingerbread for Great-granny, and one of her friends drives in, and the car knocks the ladder over, and I'm headfirst into the bushes, or I would have, like, not survived, and these people are, like, 'What did Adam do now?' Just to give you a picture of how stupid they are."

He stuck two fingers into the bag, pulling out another pair of tortilla chips. After stuffing them between his lips, he brought the beer up and tilted the can to his mouth, drinking deeply. He put the can on the floor and wiped his hands on his knees. "Every time I pinch off a loaf, she yells, 'Is someone threatening my pipes?' but man, she's the one who breaks the toilets. Her turds've gotta be the size of Mount Rushmore, and she's raggin' on me, and when I have to use the plunger, it's—forget it—the pipes in that place are, like, they hauled away shit from Moses. They're maybe older than she is. Great-granny's like eighty, and she's the one who owns the house, and boy does she let everyone know it, and she has all these friends who plow their cars into the tree out front because they get, like, cataract surgery every two days, and they're wearing these wraparound shades make 'em look like aliens, like wrinkled up aliens, and they stand next to these big old Chryslers with the smashed fronts, and they're, like, 'I need you to fix my body,' and I'm, like, 'Whoa . . . no can do.'" He laughed breathlessly for a while.

His father was listening, nodding.

With his father listening, Adam kept talking. "The mom thinks these blind people take care of me because she's always out working. She cleans offices because it pays more than cleaning houses and she can do it at night, so in the day, she does the shrimp at Mr. Meats because it pays more than slicing deli. Lookin' to that bottom line! She's the one inspired me into business school." He finished the can of beer and hopped up and got another, popping it with a quick spray while he made his way back to the sofa. "This is freedom, man."

As Ben watched him, Adam put his head down and closed his eyes. Presently, he belched from very deep within. "Aaah," he said and smiled at Ben. "So I wanted to ask you. Can I call you, like, Dad? That all right?"

"Yeah."

"I don't have a nickname."

"Okay," Ben said. There was a pause, and then Ben said, "So you're in college. You're a college boy."

"Escape from the bat cave."

"That campus. I walked through that place. I been on it."

Adam sprang up off the sofa so quickly that Ben was shot backward. "I have to show you," he said and hurried to the dining room, bringing back the laptop.

On the sofa, he opened up the computer. His fingers began flying over the keyboard. As Ben watched, the screen filled with a purple field covered with gold Qs—capital Qs and lowercase q's. Presently, the middle of the picture split, and a caped man with a mask leaped out, flashing first one way and then the other. "That's me," Adam said.

"How'd you get it to do that?"

"That's nothin'."

The letters Q-M-A-N traveled slowly under the leaping figure from right to left. Then the screen dissolved, and QMAN quivered in the middle of another background, royal blue, with a pattern of red Qs. Adam hit a button, and a large heraldic crest appeared, shield shaped and divided into four quadrants. "The Quilt family crest," Adam said.

"You're fuckin me."

"There it is."

Ben leaned forward and studied it. Two quadrants had Qs in them. The remaining two held figures a lot like the action figure that opened the website, each image posed facing out with fists at the ready. Ben

stared at it. He took in the design of colors, the ribbons that bordered
the shield, the gray feathers sticking up from the top. Inside a small
rectangle of purple that curved as though holding the feathers in place
was written in old-fashioned script, "QUILT."

"Where'd you find this?"

"Where they all come from. I drew it. Doesn't matter if your family
crest is a thousand years old. Someone sat down and drew the thing.
Back then. For the same reason. They're telling everyone, 'Hey, suckahs.
This be us!' I'm thinkin' maybe a wolf's head right dead in the center...
or a shark ... like the mouth is open and it's ... 'Chow time, suckahs'
... like that. I haven't decided. Maybe like a tiger... and maybe a paw
around each Q-man action figure. And like his face is ... killah!"

"Huh."

Adam brought a new page forward, and there was a photo of him,
sunglasses on, a hand tucked to his T-shirt like Napoleon. Around the
picture were blurbs, the kind announcing a blockbuster movie. "Q-man
rocks!" "Q-man is proud of his Quilt family heritage!" There was no
smaller print giving any reference to where they'd come from.

"I'm working on a Q-man comic," Adam said. "I'm gonna have
Q-man avenging things."

Ben stared at the screen. "The Quilt family," he said softly.

Closing the computer, Adam said, "One of the things I thought I'd
work on while I'm here."

"That's really something," Ben said.

"So what you do occupation-wise is the chef thing? You trained as
a chef?"

"Kind of. I got some training where I was. They train you in skills."
Adam leaned forward, listening.

"I got some help getting the job. Counseling stuff."

"So career-wise, this is it."

"Yeah."

"So I have to ask you," Adam said. "When did you meet, like, Mom?"

"What?" He sat back. "Jeez. Oh. I don't..... That was a long time ago."

"Nineteen ninety-seven. I could play music from that era if it helps the memory. So if you'd like, you know... to fill me in? Being my story. So. Like when did you two guys meet? How did you get introduced?"

They wouldn't have been introduced. The girls he had luck with were all running away from something. High school rebels hanging out, looking for some way to be tough and real. The college girls wouldn't have him; he was a townie and in his thirties. But the angry outlaws with fake IDs, there'd been a lot of them. Unsure of which one this might be and not about to ask for height and facial features, he tried to remember. Didn't one girl pull him aside to tell him she was pregnant? Or was he imagining one of them did because it was the last thing he'd wanted? He tried to remember a driver's license because that was his method, like he was undercover, and the trick he had, remembering the details after giving the girl's ID back, which scared them when he rattled off their information back to them. Then he'd act all protective. I'll take care of you, but you better not cross me, that sort of an act. For tough shit-kickers, those girls were really blobs of hurt.

He was afraid Adam would have a photo of her and said, quickly, "One of those things that just didn't work out. She was quite lovely. And, you know, you couldn't help being... smitten."

"So it didn't bother you that she looked Nicaraguan."

"What?"

"That's cool."

An idea appeared on Adam's face. His father read it and said, "Trust me. It's past. And you can see how it all worked out for the best, right? You're getting an education. You've got a chance with things this way."

"I guess."

"I'm just now getting back on my feet."

"What happened?"

"Good question," Ben laughed. "You don't hit bottom with a map."

"Ah," Adam laughed.

"But it's not really bottom. I'm just in reversal. Getting back up on the old steed, that's me. I had my day, though. I was in demand, oh yeah. Kind of an entrepreneur. You get a university, the market for shit is huge. You know those frat houses?"

"Yeah."

"I supplied them. I did. Those boys used to come looking for me, beggin' me for stuff, you wouldn't believe all the shit they'd buy. You could knock out an army. Send that shit to the enemy, they'd be in a coma. I used to laugh. But you got to keep your eye on the ball. If you drop the ball, you're out. So many balls in the air, you got to keep your own ball in the air. You trust someone? The law comes down on him, he slips off, and you're the guy they break down the door and yank you outta bed. And once they got a taste for you, they got an appetite for you. Just saying. As an example. But you seem to be on a good road. Anyway," he said, "you want to think about the future."

"The future."

"The past is the past," Ben told him.

"It is, yeah."

His father moved sideways and pulled out his wallet. "Here's some past. You might like this."

He separated layers of faded leather. Adam saw his father's face on a driver's license, bits of folded receipts. Rifling back under a flap, Ben pulled out a white square of stiff paper that he unfolded twice and passed to Adam. "Those are my folks. Mother, father."

Feeling his heart leap, Adam said, "Oh." He stared hard at them, his mouth open, his body poised.

A couple standing in front of a spangled quarter moon. The boy, who was very skinny, wore an ill-fitting powder-blue tuxedo and frilly shirt. He was in dark framed glasses, and his curly hair dipped slightly over the center of his forehead. The girl—Adam and Ben's face on a female teenager—also in glasses, though hers were shaped like cat's eyes, wore a low-cut yellow strapless dress overlaid with a net material that did not distract from the deep line of cleavage. Cantilevered over one breast was a corsage with two purple orchids. Initially, Adam thought he was looking at the wedding picture of his Quilt grandparents until he realized this was a prom picture. The date in small gold lettering at the bottom was 1966. There was no expression on either face. They might have only just emerged from an egg, they looked so recently hatched.

He loved them. He loved them full out. He loved them, certain they'd feel this way about him, loving him immediately and without reservation. A wave of pity rushed through him, so innocent and young did they look.

"So where are ... ?"

"Oh. Gone, yeah. They were married two months after that was taken, and after I got on the scene, he took off. He was a rover. Gambler and a rambler," Ben laughed. "And she remarried. Guy named Buddy. Then she died. Buddy married this woman, Nadine, and they had six kids. So I was kind of odd man out. They were Pentecostals. Could speak in tongues, you had to hear this stuff. No idea what they were saying. But I was like my daddy," Ben said, tapping the face in the picture, "a rambler and a gambler and a lover and a fighter. Oh, I was on the road soon as I could. I been around this country a lot."

"Yeah?"

"It's big."

"Size-wise?"

"Yeah."

Adam tried to fold the picture back up but found his hands were shaking.

"Keep it."

"Really?"

"I'll put some steaks on," Ben said. "A friend shoots deer, and I got some meat. It's in the cooler out back. We gotta cook them, or they'll go bad."

"So the stove works."

"No. It was supposed to. But I got a hibachi in the back yard and a bag of coal."

"That's a grill."

"Yeah. Like camping out."

"Awesome."

When his father went out, Adam studied the picture for a while and then looked around at the house that needed so much repair.

They ate at the card table. The steaks were huge, dark, unmarbled, gleaming with sweat, and covering a pair of plastic plates. Ben and Adam struggled with plastic knives and forks.

"Like back to the farm," Ben said in an upbeat mood. "No conveniences, but what the hell? Like the pioneers, right?"

He felt his father's embarrassment. Worse, he felt the man's cluelessness and was frightened by it.

"So, like, did the Quilts have a farm?"

"Us? A farm?"

"Way back when."

"Maybe back in Europe somewhere. Romania? Bulgaria? I forget what the original name was. Ice-backs," he laughed. "They came down from Canada. Way in the past this is. One of them was in Custer's army, so that was, like, how things went for them. For myself, I gotta say, I had some very good years. A while ago, maybe, but yeah. I did the whole . . . don't fence me in."

For a long time, they were silent, sawing through the venison that was getting cold.

"I should charge my stuff," Adam said.

"You need an outlet? I don't know if you'll get an outlet to work in here."

"Hold on. You're saying. . . . Hold on. No plug for the electronics?"

"I have to get them fixed."

"Let me get the recharger and test. I know electrical from doing sets. I lit sets for one of the plays." He hopped out of his chair. "Okay," he said, arms out as though calming an emergency. "I'll power everything down so we're good until tomorrow."

There was no electricity and no TV. Once darkness fell, Adam went up to bed. He put the prom photograph against the wall close to his bed. Alone in the room, he was awake a long time, ambient light from a streetlamp giving him a look at the islands of stain on the ceiling. The house seemed alive with tiny footsteps. Something big scurried across the roof, or in the attic itself, right over his head. He needed to urinate and didn't want to walk into that bathroom again. Taking care to be quiet, he looked for a lock on the window—there wasn't any—and tried to ease up the sash. The glass creaked and then dived forward, landing on a bush and making only a rustling sound. The sound was replicated a few moments later in a bush a few yards from the house, and he saw the shadow of something small scurrying off. Adam urinated out the window, trying to send the stream away from where it rattled against the glass.

From his garbage bag, he pulled out a heavy sweatshirt and got back into bed. Still cold from the open window, he brought the bag over his body, spreading it as an additional cover. He listened for his father and heard from the next room the labored breathing of someone still fast asleep, the dragging snore that was masculine and new to him after years with the old women at home.

Adam realized he'd been assuming things that weren't going to happen. He believed that one day after college he'd go to Thailand to visit his roommate whose father had a business and called almost nightly. Adam would play the big American who helped his bro. He'd be the good guy they might seat at the head of the table. He had believed that.

In the morning, he woke before dawn to the sound of his father driving off to work. He went downstairs with his kit and washed in the kitchen sink. When he was dressed, he walked up the hill and to the center of Harbinger and into Lou's, which was just opening. He sat down at the counter and took out his phone, thumbing his account to check the money he had. The waitress was young, possibly younger than he was, and for a moment, he stared at her, at her narrow, birdlike face and at the brown hair caught at the back of her neck and flowing down her left shoulder, curled like a cat. Her uniform hugged her as though in love with her. She walked over to him, leaning forward until he saw she wore makeup, and he liked this. It made her face beautiful.

"Don't look so bug-eyed," she said.

"No," he said and laughed. "No. I just need my coffee." Seeing her move off, he let his eyes drift down and up again. He added, "And some eggs. Please? Over easy? Is that okay?"

"Hash browns come with it," she said.

He sat forward in his seat. "Okay then," he said. "I'll have them too. Good." She was turning away, and he called after her, "What's your name?"

Turning back, she tapped her name tag with the end of her pencil. "Elle."

"Elle," he read. "You can spell it backward and forward."

She laughed.

"Madam, I'm Adam," he said.

"Very funny," she said and walked away.

"'Madam I'm Adam,' that's how I know that. Because I'm Adam. That's my name."

"Adam." She came back. "Hello, Adam."

"I don't live in Harbinger. I'm at the university. I'm in Harbinger to help my dad. My dad lives here."

"Good for him." She began turning away again.

"Elle backward and forward. Do you get that a lot?"

She put her hand flat on the counter in front of him and leaned in his direction. "Nope. Now, do you want anything else?" She grinned at him.

"Yeah. Yeah, I do. Is there, like, an outlet I can use? My phone's almost dead."

She took his phone and the recharger he was pulling from his pocket. He watched her long, thin fingers play around them for a moment before she turned and, bending to look down the length of the counter, she spotted a plug and went over to it without hurrying, looking back at him once before shoving the recharger in fast. She put his phone carefully on the counter and gave him a smile.

"Oh," he said very softly. She was walking away again. He called to her, "Do you happen to know, is there, like, a hardware store? Nearby?"

"Around the corner and down a block," she said.

"I'm helping my dad fix up his new house. I'm pretty good at fixing things."

She came back to him, leaning even closer this time and said, like a secret only he should hear, "You know, I need to put your order in if you want to eat."

He laughed too loud at that.

She was gone for a while and returned when a couple came in and sat at the far end of the counter. He watched her talking to them with a feeling of distress that they had her attention. His phone pinged, and he got up and retrieved it, holding it high when she turned so she could see it was charged. She came back and, looking pleased with herself, stayed busy near his place, wiping the counter and filling ketchup bottles.

He asked, "So. You work here?"

"No."

He laughed.

She said, "Only in the mornings. I go to class in the afternoon. I'm in medical administration."

"Oh yeah?"

"That's where the jobs are."

"You should give me your number. I'm in business. Hospitals are business."

She reached into her pocket and brought out her phone. Holding it in both hands near her heart, she gave him a long, critical look. Finally, she said, "Okay."

He called out his number, watching her punch it in.

As daylight through the windows grew stronger and the aroma of brewing coffee reached them from the other end of the counter, Adam and Elle remained poised above their phones, thumbing quickly. Photos and texts were sent up into whatever tower was nearby and then over and back to the other phone, Elle and Adam rocking slightly, each bent over a screen, Adam capturing Elle, this number and these images of her, holding her in his hand even as she stood in front of him, pressing her own keyboard.

When his food came, he felt too excited to eat. Other customers came in, and she went to wait on them. He tried not to keep looking around for her.

On his way back to the house with the packages from the hardware store, he recalculated his money so he could eat breakfast there every morning. Wasn't she beautiful, he thought. Beautiful, the word rang in his head. He opened the door to the house and saw something small race across the floor and out through a hole under the baseboard. Investigating the hole, he found the wood around it soft. The house looked solid to him, but now he walked around, knocking here and there on a wall or touching the frame of a window, and felt wood sinking under his touch, spongy.

He noticed again the papers from Red Sled Realty that his father had left on the mantel. In the bright daylight, he read through them carefully. His father had put down five thousand on a forty-thousand-dollar loan. Or it was a kind of loan. Rent to buy seemed the arrangement. The interest rate was twelve percent. Adam frowned. Mortgage rates were around three percent that year. Twelve seemed high. On a separate sheet were stipulations. The place had to be up to code in four months. If not, the money was forfeit, and his father would be evicted. Four months seemed a long time, though. He opened the plastic bags he'd carried home from Harbinger Hardware and took the new fuses and lines of number twelve wire and the tools he'd bought. Then he ran upstairs to his bedroom and taped plastic over his window until he could get it repaired. With the wiring equipment, he went downstairs to the basement.

It wasn't as bad as he'd feared. Unfinished, with damp and mold on the walls, it contained a smell he couldn't identify until he saw a small heap of animal droppings. Coming in from the cold, he supposed and hoped for only mice rather than rats. There was an old furnace and water heater freckled with rust. The fuse box was near the bottom of the stairs, and he took the cover off and looked things over. Fifteen amps and only a handful of fuses. The old wire would be strung up around knobs and he could fish up some of the new wire after connecting it to twenty-amp fuses. He shut down the electrical switch for the house. The furnace, the only thing working in the house, went off with a sigh. He replaced the old fuses, sliced open yellow Romex with a knife blade and then stripped the hot and neutral wires. He used the plastic bag from the hardware store to keep his tools together and to help carry everything upstairs.

In the kitchen, he opened up an outlet, pulled the box out, and took a length of stiff wire to fish up the number twelve from below. He had some luck. It wouldn't last long, he knew, and he went upstairs to feed new wire down the soil stack. Working quickly, he replaced the kitchen outlets and plugged in his computer to charge it. When he went into the dining room, he unscrewed the outlet cover, and part of the wall came off with it. He pressed his fingers around the hole. The plaster gave under slight pressure. He thought it felt damp, held up by the wallpaper. When he touched the stud just to the side of it, it crumbled in his hand, an ochre color and less wood than particles. See about that later, he thought and found a route along the knobs for more wire.

About midafternoon, he stepped back to survey how the first floor looked. A large hole gaped in the dining room wall that he knew could be filled with plasterboard, but he was able to turn on the lights of the chandelier.

Outside, he rescued the glass that had fallen out of his window. Dotted with dried urine and broken in two corners, it seemed intact enough to use. He washed it under the outside tap. Upstairs, he put it back into the wooden framing and taped it enough to hold it. Before he was finished, he heard a buzzing, thrumming noise. He put his hand flat against the wall and moved slowly along one wall and then the next. When a section of wall vibrated under his hand, he drew the hand away. It was sticky with honey. There was an outlet near the baseboard. He unscrewed the cover and a bee emerged, golden and floating upward like a liquid bubble in the afternoon light. Another bee followed and was followed in turn by two more bees and then a few more after that.

Adam stepped back as they continued filling his bedroom. Quickly he undid the windowpane, resting the broken glass on the floor. He ducked low and hurried out to the hallway, shutting the door behind him. The buzzing increased. Adam ran downstairs and outside to watch them emerge from the house.

He was standing near the driveway when his father returned from work. The older man got out of the car. "You're still here, huh?"

It was a joke Adam didn't like. He felt it sounded pathetic. "So that's what I was hearing," Ben said, spotting the bees.

"They made honey," Adam told him.

"Inside?" Ben asked. "Maybe you could sell the stuff." He saw one of the bees land on his elbow and beat at it with his free hand. "Off. Get off me!" he hollered, skipping backward. When he turned, he spotted a herd of deer a few yards away.

They looked back at him from the low bushes, whose branches were exposed after a sunny day.

"Yearrrgh!" he yelled at them and ran with his arms waving up and down.

They stared at him until he grew close to them, at which point, they turned their tails to him and bounded away. Ben kept running after them, his arms flailing, finally tripping and falling forward. He got back up, wiping at his knees and yelling, "God fucking damn it!"

Adam stared after his father.

Ben returned and walked over to the hibachi in the backyard where a few bees had landed. He kicked the hibachi hard, but it was heavy enough that it only jumped a few feet and landed on its side.

"All right," Ben said. He hobbled. "All right. Fuckin bees." He walked away toward the edge of the property like a student made to stand in the corner. He urinated. Zipping up, he came back toward the house. "Hey, Adam," he called. "So we're still here. Hey. How'd your day go? Huh?"

Adam didn't think his father really wanted to know. He followed the man into the house and then from room to room. "Holy shit," Ben said. "Yeah, I'm gonna get to these things. Fix it up. So yeah, this is good.

You're really making a start. Well, all right." In the living room Ben fell backward onto the sofa and sat there breathing in loud short breaths. "What are you gonna do, right? What is anyone ever gonna do?"

"I could call out for a pizza," Adam said.

Ben hitched leftward to one hip and reached back and pulled out his wallet. His large face bent over the narrow leather gills. From the depths, he pulled out a twenty, folded to the size of a stick of gum. Silently he handed it to Adam, then let his head knock back against the sofa.

"Long day?" Adam asked, taking the money.

"Same old." Ben's eyes were closed.

It was dark out when they ate under the dining room chandelier that Ben kept glancing up at as though the wagon wheel might fall and land on the pizza.

I was wondering, Adam kept beginning inside his head to coax information from his father. Information or advice. Or any kind of attention. He edited what he might say and then looked at his father, who appeared so tired he had trouble holding up his slice of pizza. I was wondering. This girl. A girl in town. So what do you think?

His father had fallen asleep at the table. Gently, he went over and shook him and led him upstairs, where he collapsed onto the mattress in the big bedroom. Adam covered him and then tucked the blankets and sheets around him.

When the bees quieted down for the night, Adam slipped into his room and removed the futon and his bags, taking them into the smallest of the three bedrooms. On his phone, he texted Elle and waited only a few moments before she replied. So much to tell her, the bees for one thing. His coming work in the school's theater department as a set builder was another, and this seemed to fascinate her. From there, he was on to his business classes, giving her the idea that he was soon to be a powerful mogul.

"How is your dad?" she asked.

"Okay," he thumbed quickly and brought the exchange to an end.

Ancestry

"WE MET IN PRISON," George told their friends.

"In Paris," Mackenzie added. "So, you know, romantic."

This was their story after they'd married and moved back to the States.

"She looked amazing behind bars," he said.

In fact they'd met in the hallway in front of a police inspector's office a floor above the cell of George's client, but that didn't sound as good. And they inflated their odd-couple appearance.

"I was still jet-lagged," he said. "I looked like an unmade bed." She was slim, in a black dress. "She made me want to light up a cigarette. And I don't smoke."

Four years older, she was also a few inches taller. He had a pair of divorces and two boys in college. "So, obviously, made for each other."

• • •

She had spotted him in the busy police station as an American. His clothes identified him, as well as the way he stood, hands in his pockets, silent amid that frothy language, a face expressing ownership, although for what would be anyone's guess.

"Are you Carl's father?"

He'd given a start. "I'm his lawyer. You are . . . ?"

"Mackenzie Tolen. I'm with the embassy."

"Can you get him out?" He'd smiled at her. "Save me the trouble."

She shook her head. "I offer tranquility. The French are in charge of the liberty part."

"Tranquility," he'd repeated as though he'd never heard the word before.

They were guided downstairs by a police inspector who remembered her from previous visits. French was exchanged, friendly, rapid-fire. George leaned toward them as though proximity would help him make out what was being said.

When she turned in his direction, he had moved too close. "Sorry," he murmured, giving her room.

She told him, "Your client will need a French advocate. I can give you a list of bilingual ones."

"Is the charge very serious?"

"It's criminal," she said.

Later, he'd describe meeting her as "a little frightening. I had to up my game. Which wasn't easy since I didn't have a game."

She knew she could appear stiff. On her arrival a year earlier as a consular officer, she'd depended on strict discipline to rouse her from an inclination to self-pity and move her out smartly every morning and carry her through a long day with her small office overstuffed with file cabinets, phones ringing, an inbox ever refilling, the entire American embassy bustling, the Dayton Accords soon to be signed, meetings and dinners to be planned, the public rooms intimidating, the guest lists heart-stopping, research into who was exactly which diplomat and how to pronounce the name, something she must never get wrong.

She'd started life as a lazy and obnoxious little girl too aware she lacked brains or coordination, money or talent. She was tall and homely, very tall and exceedingly homely, understanding early how little she had to make her way in the world. Then one day, she learned that she did have an exceptional attribute after all.

Her mother told her, "You and I are descendants of the Dalzells." The name was slurred in her mother's pronunciation to sound like Dazzle.

Mackenzie had heard the name mentioned before but without reference. It could have been a distant cousin living in a different part of the country. Her mother had a lot to say about this long-dead Scottish lord while she sat on the back stoop just after Mackenzie's father had abandoned them, her head high in spite of the trembling hands and breaking voice. Mackenzie, ten at the time, was to understand this ancestor was strong. "Disciplined" was the word her mother landed on like a hammer.

"He wasn't someone to quit or run away. No. He was a warrior. Someone who'd *stick*. He would *never* give up."

There was no fortune, she'd understood. The life of Dazzle had occurred too long ago and too far away. Maybe if she'd been eight, a fantasy might have emerged, and she'd believe herself a princess. Had she been a teenager, the story of an esteemed ancestor would have inspired incredulity and a sneer. Her mother, after all, lived for romance novels and wine. But at ten, she was a perfect receptacle. Desire had always gripped her, but it was nebulous beyond the hope she might one day leave home and have a life. Now she seized on this ghost for inspiration.

With Dazzle in mind, she applied herself at school. Slowly and then with increasing dedication, she pushed herself forward. In time, she stopped calling on this imagined soul because his influence had become her character. At work, she was seen as bracingly self-assured and competent. She was encouraged to take tests and advance. After testing into the State Department she completed the A-100 training and learned French. She found she loved her work, loved the friends she made among her colleagues. Tucked under her sleeve, she kept two wristwatches, one on Washington time, the other for her posting, Algeria to begin with, Cyprus and Vietnam to follow. By the time she met George in Paris, she had two more languages under her belt and a human resources file full of praise but no love life. She'd soldiered on through an early and dismal affair, after which there'd been a string of near misses. Her sexual highway lacked signage, and now here was this George, announcing who he was with his tourist clothes and an expression of ownership.

Approaching Carl's cell, she told him, "Be sure he understands he'll have to go before a judge."

"I'm aware of judges," he assured her.

In the meantime, the two of them got a look at Carl. He was eighteen, small, dwarfed by a tent of thick brown hair. Loud, too, as he played to an imaginary audience somewhat behind and above the actual humans present, of which there were five. His "Christ!" as George and Mackenzie squeezed in was also played to the balcony.

An American woman at the back of the cell, bracketed by two associates, introduced herself as Carl's lawyer.

"I'm Carl's lawyer," George told her.

"Really?" Carl asked the room. "Seriously?"

It appeared Carl's divorced parents avoided communication, and Kathy—her name—and George had been hired from different law firms in different states and rushed over on competing airlines.

The French moved out to the hallway, departing with amusement, quickly.

Carl looked up at Mackenzie. "Are you another lawyer? Or are you the guns and money?"

Mackenzie explained she was only there to look out for an American citizen.

"I'm a citizen of the *world*," Carl said.

"The charge says you tried to steal medals from the museum of—"

"No!" Carl said. "It was performance art. I was protesting. I'm anti-war. That makes me a political prisoner. And anyway, I didn't steal anything. I wasn't able to unhook them. No crime, folks, nothing to look at here, keep moving."

Mackenzie noted the time and the condition of the cell. She'd expected exactly what she found. In another part of the world, she might have discovered something sinister, but not here. George went into the corridor to confer with Kathy and the two associates who'd flown over with her.

Mackenzie sat down next to Carl, who said, "I thought this city liked art."

She had a few questions for him: "Do you have any money? Any way to call your parents?"

"My money was stolen. Get them to wire money to me. You've got their phone number, right? Call them."

"I can do that."

"Finally. Something."

Then George returned with Kathy. George told Carl, "They're going to get you an advocate. Someone who speaks English." Then he said to Mackenzie, "Kathy wants to handle it."

Mackenzie nodded, eager to be off. To Kathy, she said, "I'll ask his parents to wire money."

Kathy told her, "They already did. I'm getting it for him."

"You can both do it," Carl said. "They can wire it twice. Hey. One of you ask my dad and the other ask my mom. Do it that way."

After George and Mackenzie concluded with the police, they walked out together.

"Can she get him released?" she asked.

"Would anyone want to?"

He looked around for a cab, but she steamed forward, and he fell into step beside her.

"He's not the usual," she said. "I've been over to see some who have no resources, no family money, no understanding of the charges." She looked at him. "Are you very good at what you do?"

The question surprised him, and it took a moment before he gave a resounding yes, laughing. They continued on, talking easily to each other until she realized how relaxed she felt in his company.

In time they were in the Latin Quarter and he sighed for the buildings that had been cleaned and brightened, the ghosts of the twenties scattered.

"I once thought I'd be a writer," he said. "The *Moveable Feast* moved on before I got here. I was going to write the great American novel."

"Oh my."

"Was this your plan? This job? Working in Paris?"

"Me? I wanted to be a jockey. I was going to win the Kentucky Derby." He glanced up at her. "And how come that didn't work out?"

She smiled at him. "I never learned how to ride."

"Well, don't lose the dream. Where are we?"

"I was following you," she said. "Actually we're in the direction of the river. "Sort of on our way home."

"Maybe lunch?"

A few blocks later, she guided him across an intersection and into La Fourmi Ailée. She ordered two champagnes and wondered if she'd lost her mind. It was the middle of the day, and she was due back in her office.

"I suppose it's five o'clock somewhere," he said, taking in the shelves of books, the teapots, the booth near the wall where a young couple leaned toward each other, moony-eyed.

"Are Carl's parents rich?" she asked.

"Mom is. Dad is broke. He's a friend. I told him I'd take a look." He grinned at her. "I always wanted an excuse to come back. It's been a long time." He checked his forehead for sweat, greeted the champagne with enthusiasm when it arrived.

"What's it like to defend criminals?"

"Interesting, but financially ridiculous," he said. "You have to get the money up front. If they won't pay taxes, they're not inclined to pay you. And that was most of my work, tax cheats. But I know enough criminal law. Not that I'm needed here any longer. I just want to be able to tell my friend his kid will be all right, well not all right, I guess. Defended. What a stupid. . . . Trying to steal medals?"

"Napoleon's medal is the size of a saucer and covered in little diamonds."

"How did he even get near it?"

"He didn't. They have good security. It's the museum across from the d'Orsay. It's nice. Musée de la Légion d'honneur. They don't charge to get in."

"That explains a lot. I was surprised the arrest wasn't for vagrancy." To her questioning face, he said, "Or drugs. The mother sent him here to clean up his act."

"Paris as tough love? Really?"

He laughed. "Poor Carl."

She felt no sympathy for Carl. There was a lesson she'd learned working in embassies: people of import in the world, people with real agency, had surprising humility. The loudmouths were never worth attending. She could live without Carl but for the fact that he was the reason she met this very likeable man.

He said, "The last time I was over here, I went to Normandy. I love that stuff."

He described his interest in military history as an escape from his clients. As the law caught up with them, they showed little beyond irritation at being booted from some difficult game at which they'd grown skillful. For relief from thinking about them, he read up on the Great War, the Civil War, the American Revolution. He asked Mackenzie if she knew where Lafayette was buried.

"It's not in town. Picpus Cemetery. It's out a ways." Seeing the look he gave her, she added, surprising herself, "I'm sure we could find it."

• • •

Later, back in the States, George would tell the story of how they got lost.

"That's when I knew Mackenzie never gave up. Nothing daunted this woman. That was when I knew I had to marry her. We took off Saturday morning, and I thought we'd end up in Italy or something. I would've thrown in the towel. And then we finally got off at the right stop, and there's construction all over the place. It's way the heck out of the city. She's asking everyone where it is. No one knows. She translates this for me, it's hopeless, and then she says, 'But don't worry. I think we're close.'"

They were. Beyond a pair of ancient doors. To enter the grounds was to step back hundreds of years. They wandered, watched by a chicken near an old church. Behind the church were fields and, under the grass, mass graves from the Revolution. The quiet and the sense of eternity arrested them. From here, they could see the entrance in a far wall that led to the raised crypts. She felt George's hand at the back of her head and leaned forward with a wild shake of her heart to take his lips on hers.

He moved out of his hotel into her apartment. He didn't go home. The excuse was to wait for Carl's release. But Carl's mother and her connections managed to have her boy sprung more quickly than George felt diplomatic. So he stayed to avoid feeling like an Ugly American and then stayed for some vacation time—as long as he was here anyway. And then he stayed because they'd never actually gone into the walled-off part of the cemetery where Lafayette was interred. Once they'd started kissing, they'd turned around and hurried back. And he could hardly leave Paris without finding Picpus again and doing his *Nous sommes ici*, and then he stayed because they were able to arrange a marriage in France. And then he stayed an additional week as Mackenzie finalized her exit from the embassy so she could go home with him.

Shortly before leaving Paris, she happened to be looking at the name Dalzell on a list for an upcoming reception when her colleague read it off. The Z was treated like a Y. DeYell. For God's sake, she thought.

It was her job to know pronunciations and titles and honorifics. Why hadn't she ever looked up her own ancestor?

She touched very gently the name. "I'm related to them."

"The Dalzells? Oh my."

"Very distant. They wouldn't know me."

But seeing the name on the list moved her. She had leaned on this family to keep heart. She didn't want to imagine where she might have ended up without knowing she connected to them. Now she felt protective of these descendants, working late on the finer details of the reception, possibly smoothing a wrinkle they might have otherwise encountered.

"I wasn't there that night, but I tried to find some pictures and maybe see what they looked like." She mentioned to George that one day the two of them should visit Scotland.

But once home, they never traveled. Work kept them both very busy. And they were low on funds. She supported her mother, whose care grew increasingly expensive as dementia took her. Divorces and the education of his boys had sapped his savings. Mackenzie wanted a relationship with George's sons, but though the younger boy was kind, the elder one made no secret he found her weird and his father silly. Time with him left her exhausted. And people were always coming by. Their friends stopped in often and liked to stay late, hanging out as though afraid to leave.

Why? she wondered, until one of them said, "You're happy. Both of you. Everybody else I know is so angry."

But a few years after they'd both retired, their doors closed. Mackenzie had health problems and George was dying. People still came by but to check on them.

A few months after George's funeral, her closest friend found her in the dining room with travel information on Scotland spread all over the table. She was agitated and busy with decisions on car hire and places to stay.

"How else can I stand it? Everything's gone out of me. When I met George, I thought all the shit I went through had a purpose. I'm thinking if I go to Scotland, I'll begin to feel better. More myself."

"You wouldn't rather go to Paris?"

"Oh my God, the memories would kill me. George is *gone*. I couldn't bear seeing those streets again. No, I need to walk around Scotland."

George would know to find her there. He'd meet her in some form or other. She was certain of it.

"You're going by yourself?"

"People do that all the time," she said. "I *want* to go alone."

The trip was for communion, not photographs.

She went to Edinburgh and it rained. It was August and the Festival Fringe was on. A roistering crowd of the young and hopeful kept her off balance. Under assault from umbrellas, she found a side street and hurried up a steep hill for some relief. It was too steep for her. She turned again along a lane that seemed level.

As she tried to catch her breath, she happened to spot a girl of about ten. The girl looked back at her in such a way that Mackenzie saw her childhood self and recalled the moment she'd realized her dad would not be home again, that he didn't want her and had abandoned her. The stab of memory took her so vividly she reeled. The girl turned and was gone. Mackenzie fled back to the main street. The rain stopped and the crowd grew bigger. She took refuge in a pub. Festival people came in after her and pressed publicity flyers on her. By the time the waiter began suggesting ales, or perhaps malts, her defenses were down, and she said yes to anything and everything and was soon drunk. Driving away from Edinburgh, she almost got into an accident.

"The other driver cursed at me," she told her friends after getting home. "I can't understand why the trip was such a disaster."

As she grew older, losing purchase on the here and now, she felt more acutely the net of circumstance and coincidence. How had so many odd occurrences delivered her into that police station just as George arrived? The chance of their running into each other was so extraordinary, surely it had been arranged from the beyond. By whom? By someone aware of the price of sticking it out? Someone who'd wanted to reward her, a mystery as otherworldly as that first kiss above a field of bones.

A year before she died, she received a DNA test from the younger of her stepsons as a Christmas present. They had recently become available. She was depressed and suffered from macular degeneration. Nothing else presented itself as so clearly a means to cheer her up, which it did. She was childish with anticipation. The results showed she was mostly Danish, fifty-eight percent, with sixteen percent Croatian and twelve percent Italian. The few minor notes were Greek, European Jew, and Hawaiian. In the shocked silence that followed, her stepson added one percent Scottish, in a loud voice, since by then, she was almost as deaf as she was blind.

The Punch

THE FIRST THING Joan did after she punched Paul Hedges was dunk her hand into her water glass. The ice water soothed her fingers all the way up to the knuckles. Her knuckles were what had smashed against the solid rock of Paul's jaw. But in spite of the pain, she rang with bliss. Every cell in her body sang with ecstasy over what she'd just done, and kept singing in the high octaves. Was she sitting on this chair? She was levitating, wasn't she? It was a feeling like no other.

For the people who'd been looking in her direction at the time, there was a momentary collective holding of breath. Had they just witnessed a woman fly up and punch Paul, who'd then disappeared toward the floor? Or had he stumbled and fallen? That had to be it: *He tripped and fell just as Joan got out of her chair, right?* Others in the room were now looking over, murmuring, *What happened? Did something just happen?*

She hadn't imagined herself a woman who would ever actually punch anyone. Not at a gala dinner. Not at this gala dinner, which was for artists under thirty whose work addressed social issues. One of those artists, Tobruk, was at their table. What kind of message was she sending?

At fifty-five, she had received a warning from her doctor about her osteopenia and the need for exercise. That was three years ago. Resistance training was paramount. "You have the shoulders of an eighty-year-old. Play tennis."

Then I'll have the knees of an unstrung racket, she thought. She didn't want to play tennis.

Instead, she used the body bag at the gym. Folding towels around her hands to mimic gloves, she let fly. Each blow felt like bone mass delivered straight to her spongy shoulders. Thirty, forty, fifty reps.

"I'm getting good at this," she'd told Don, her husband.

He sucked in his stomach and told her to have a go. Instinctively she faked with her right and landed a blow near his kidney with her left.

"You *are* good. Jesus." He left the room, holding his side.

Don wasn't at the gala. He was in Philadelphia doing research. After being let go by his newspaper and finding no other job, he'd decided to write a book on the American Revolution. Joan had encouraged him.

"People love the forefathers. And don't forget the foremothers."

Her restaurant was doing all right. Not great, but the bills got paid. Their kids were out of college and on their own, her son after a few postgraduate years in the basement. He was still lost, but now he was living off his girlfriend. Perhaps with the men in her life out of work she'd gone alpha? Perhaps she wasn't really very nice? Beyond that, it was a mystery to her why she'd leapt from her seat in her floor-length, second-hand Chanel—a find at the Somerset Hills Visiting Nurse Association Rummage—and cold-cocked a man twice her size.

Paul Hedges was the one who'd arranged for her neighborhood grammar school to be closed and the land and building put on the market. It was Paul who'd then bought it cheap and converted the building into condos. But that was three years ago and even Joan had to admit there were no little children in the neighborhood anymore. She hoped there would be in the future and wanted the school kept open, ready for them. But when she jumped up and punched him, the grammar school had been far from her mind.

It was his face. It was the way he sneered at her, as though he'd seen her in the open dressing room behind the boutique section when she'd wriggled into the gently worn Chanel and realized it fit. But he looked at everyone that way.

She thought she'd broken some bones. When her fingers felt better, felt freezing in fact, she pulled out her hand and dried it with her napkin. Now the sharp stab was replaced by a throbbing ache. But none of her pain distracted her from the exhilaration still on her. Shaking with happiness, she felt spectacular.

"I slipped," he told the friends who'd rushed over to help him. His shoes made a scrabbling noise as he hurriedly got back on his feet. "It's nothing," he said. When they protested, he yelled, "I said I slipped!"

She heard this but didn't look his way. Sorry wasn't offered by her. She felt a little sorry for her knuckles.

"I'm fine," Paul said. "I was way off balance."

Hah, she thought.

"Did you see that nutty old lady?" he laughed.

Unless she began belting everyone in the room, the ecstasy would fade, which it had already begun doing. Some giddiness remained. She would soon be back to her old self, Joan Connors, owner of the Pleiades restaurant, wearing a sample-size beige silk that was cut so well it felt like pajamas and made her feel like Cleopatra. She could see Paul and his friends walking toward the front of the room as though all was well.

There seemed a shift in the atmosphere around her. She had acquaintances throughout the large room, but her closest friends were sitting beside her. Annette had bought the table for all of them. Joan imagined the price had been huge. It was an award ceremony. Like most people who ran a business and didn't paint pictures or create novels, she loved people like Tobruk, who was to the right of Annette and recently back from the front of the room, where he'd been given a check for thirty-five thousand dollars. Joan sighed at the expression Tobruk wore the whole night. *When we nonartists love you, why do you look like you're suffering anal cramps? Hmm?*

None of her friends met her eye. The thrill that electrified her at the moment she punched Paul ebbed. My God, she thought, it's almost gone. After fizzing with intense ringing, singing from head to toe, now there was nothing much at all. When she looked from friend to even closer friend, she wanted eye contact. She needed understanding.

About to say something to them—*Did I cross a line?*—she was distracted by a large, bald man at the next table, who rose and came over to her. He moved like someone signaling that his tuxedo was a ruse and his life full of awesome feats in case John Le Carré or Alan Furst was sitting at a nearby table, discretely observing him—wanting to give the spy novelists some meat. From the table behind her, he grabbed an empty chair, ignoring the quick hand of the woman sitting beside it that collected the purse on it.

He parked the chair close to Joan's and leaned toward her, speaking in a low voice something like, "He had it coming." Or maybe it was, "Good for you."

She didn't hear what he said because she was already talking to him. She had turned with authority toward him, surprising herself with how loud she was. "What was I supposed to do, right?" She said this like someone who ran numbers instead of a restaurant with a back room for hosting baby showers. "He was askin' for it." Speaking tough brought back a little of the ecstasy that had thrilled her during and just after landing her punch. Only a reminder of the sensation, it was at least something.

Unsure of who this new Joan was, she turned back to her friends, presenting again the woman they'd known since high school. *Yes, it's me!* These friends, the very people around her diverting their gaze, had always gathered to her side when she'd been low. She believed the Pleiades restaurant she'd created—a bright, busy place in Montclair, full of mismatched, comfortable furniture—was an homage to them.

She smiled at them now. But they looked elsewhere.

She felt the large hand of the man in the spy-game tux settle against the lower back of her chair. "These fuckers," he said, his mouth close to her ear. "Overage frat boys. You made my day. I think I'm in love, if you believe that shit." His laugh was a kind of snort. As he got up, his large hand patted a few times the rump of her chair and he returned to his table.

At her own table, her friends still refused to look at her, though their eyes were now wide with alarm. It seemed these friends had heard her talk like a noir villain. She gave a light laugh as though she were more surprised by her behavior than anyone.

Movement nearby caught her attention. The large, bald man was arguing with a woman at his table, or at least the woman was arguing; the bald man was laughing at her. Joan took his side of the fight. Why? she wondered. He was someone she wouldn't have wanted in her restaurant, someone who couldn't appreciate local sourcing. He loved her, if she believed that shit.

He would not be her only champion that evening. Madeleine Wrightwater came up to her when she went out to the hallway for the ladies room. Madeleine was wearing a dress that would've had Joan's mother sighing and going, "Tsk," back when Joan's mother was still compos mentis and Joan and Don weren't paying for her assisted living. Madeleine's dress had an aggressive décolletage with the fabric edged in rhinestones, making a kind of runway for her shaking cleavage. In front of the sign for women, Madeleine did a slight jump and popped her fist in the air.

"My hero!" Grabbing Joan's shoulders, she pulled her toward the rhinestones, saying, "You did what I wanted to do when he got me fired. He said I looked like a dog. He told me he was afraid I'd hump his leg."

Joan pulled back and pointed a finger toward the toilets.

Madeleine released her, saying, "He's so effing arrogant. Yaaay, Joan!"
Joan walked into the women's room with Madeleine calling after
her, "Tell me who's next. I want to hold your purse."

Joan remained in the stall longer than she needed. When she
emerged, she went to the last sink by the wall. Her knuckles still ached,
and she spent a lot of time moving her good hand in front of the black
remote window to start and then start again the water over the injured
knuckles. A knuckle sandwich. A belt in the kisser. Kapow. *You wanna
piece a dis? You want a knuckle sammich? Hah?*

What a strange evening it's been.

A few women came in, and Joan was aware of the sudden arrest of
their conversation. They ducked into stalls. She decided to ignore them
and dried her hands and left.

As she walked to her table, she had the sense of being invisible and
yet the focus of everyone's attention. It was late enough in the evening
that people were starting to leave. Those on their way out ignored her
as well. Joan told herself not to care. They were acquaintances. Her own
table, with her own friends—this was different. *Guys? You guys!* Guys
didn't seem the right word. *Ladies?* Worse. It had such a phony ring
when she practiced it in her head.

She said, "Maria?" and smiled. Maria shut her eyes. "Suzanne?" Suzanne shook her head. Joan said, "Well that was a shock. I mean, I can't
imagine what came over me."

Suzanne and Tony, her husband, once he stopped inspecting the
ceiling, stood and walked out. Vanessa and Annette were standing and
said goodbye to Maria.

What Joan noticed about her friends was how tired they seemed.
She understood why. She had just yanked out a wall of social sandbags
that kept out the endless river of life's shit. They had enough shit to deal
with already, thank you very much. Maria got up. So did Raf, Maria's
husband, and Tobruk. It was Tobruk who looked over at Joan before
leaving. He seemed only curious.

Before she'd punched Paul, the women had been laughing about how long they'd been calling themselves, along with two who hadn't been able to join them that evening, the seven sisters.

She was alone at the table. The table now looked enormous. She thought it might be good to get up. Quickly, she thought, leave this place. *Git the fuck outta heah.* But she felt weighted by lead. A lead ass. My God, maybe I'm dying, and I'll just leave my body and fly up where it won't matter. She waited. But she didn't die.

A woman approached her, looking deeply concerned. "What did he do?" she asked.

"Who?"

"Paul."

"Oh. I guess the way he turned the grammar school into condos."

"I meant just now."

"He called Madeleine Wrightwater a dog."

"No, I mean just before you hit him."

"Well, he was arrogant."

"He's always been arrogant."

"Exactly."

"What did he say?"

"Well, it wasn't a word. It was the way he looked at me. Down his nose."

"He didn't assault you?"

"I assaulted him. I think you know that."

"But why?"

"The truth, honey? I knew I could take him. Just then. He was in position and I had him. Awright? One second later, no way. So it was, hey, go for it or lose it. I mean, Whatdaya want? He was blocking my fucking view. Should I put up with that?"

The woman turned and hurried toward the other end of the room.

Joan rose and walked out to the building's foyer.

She thought the main door was heavier than it was and her pull made it bang when it flew open. The couple at the bottom of the stairs turned and, seeing Joan, brought their arms up defensively, yelling, "Don't hit me! Don't hit me!" They laughed uproariously as they walked toward the parking lot.

In the car going home, the silky skirt of her gown tucked around her knees, Joan realized she was punching the steering wheel of her Outback with the edge of her good hand. This hurt. But she wanted to punch someone. Punch. Punch. Punch. That moment of bliss wasn't returned. It wouldn't come back. And she wanted to feel it again so badly.

"What bothers me is that I can't justify punching him. There was no start to it. I just did it. Why?"

"I'm not your therapist. I'm not your lawyer either, because Paul might sue you, though I don't think he will. He didn't press charges, right? My take was that Paul got up from the floor and didn't want anyone to think a woman flattened him. What I'm concerned about is the video. Someone recorded it, but only the end. Paul is on the floor, and you look a bit goddess-like. It's the dress. But there's something odd about the clip. It looks staged. Which means a lot of people won't believe it. And the actual moment of contact wasn't recorded. So that's very lucky."

"Annette, I'm trying to tell you the problem I'm having. No one's coming into the restaurant since it happened. There's a social media boycott. Twenty years, I built that restaurant from nothing. I remember sweeping the floor and painting the walls. My staff gets medical insurance, that's how good things were going. Now it's empty. The Pleiades is our only income until Don gets his book sold. If he gets it sold."

"That's the first thing then. We remake the restaurant."

"I thought a cookbook based on the menu."

"Oh God no, not with your name and picture on it, are you serious? No, we have to untangle you from the property."

"But I created the Pleiades."

"And now it can't breathe. You're strangling it. You have to let it go."

"But I love it."

"All the more reason."

Annette's contract was in front of her. Joan tried to read through it and couldn't focus. "I have no money. I'm paying my staff from our retirement account."

"I don't want your money. What we do is give my agency a cut of the future profits. That's how confident I am in what I can do for you."

After signing the papers, Joan went downstairs and out to the street. A young man walking toward the building met her eye. He then glanced away and gave her a wide berth. She could remember being young and men regarding her. This was different. He's afraid of me. A thrill took her from head to toe.

"Women's stories are big now, so I decided to do the biography of Mary Ludwig Hays McCauley. You might know her as Molly Pitcher. A hero of the American Revolution. And what a woman. This was a gal who punched above her weight. Before I had her biography finished, I had a movie deal." Don was talking to the small crowd at the launching party for his book. It was held in the second Pleiades just after it opened in Hoboken.

Their son was running the restaurants now, and the whimsical mismatched furniture had been replaced by movie posters of romantic comedies and stainless steel. The wings and sliders he put on the menu dovetailed with the copy Annette wrote to introduce new management and a self-service vibe: "If there's a chance for some heat, meet at the coolest place around." The Pleiades became the spot to schedule dating app possibilities and "check each other out." People started calling it the "Please-a me." A third Pleiades would open soon in Long Branch. Joan wasn't at the book party, though from the outset, she'd been relieved that Don had sold his book and that their son was no longer lost.

It wasn't quite a week after the book party that she heard Don's heavy step each time he answered the door. They were assembling in the living room, her friends, her grown children. Filtering down through the hardwood floor were serious voices, voices of concern. She remained on the old sofa her son had brought into the basement when he was between things and living with them.

All his video games were still here. After the cast came off her hand, she'd begun playing them. It seemed therapeutic, something to prevent adhesions in her wrist and fingers. After she'd played them many times, advancing in expertise, she began buying new ones. *Call of Duty*. *Battlefield*. She torqued and blasted and bammed, kapow, kapow. All fake thrills, but as close as she could get to that moment when she'd punched Paul.

From the sound of all the footsteps, there were a lot of them getting ready to come downstairs and have a talk with her. *Just a conversation.* It wouldn't be the first. *We all love you. That's why we want to help you. We love you so much.* Yeah, right, if I can believe that shit. The game was almost finished. If they stayed upstairs for a while, for Don to maybe put out some snacks and maybe for all of them to figure out how they'd approach her, she'd have time for another game. Another game and then maybe a race upstairs to the shower? One more game and she promised herself she'd wash her hair. There might be some shirts that were clean. And if her feet were washed, it wouldn't matter that she was barefoot. The trouble was, she wished so very much that she could put on something that wasn't food-stained, that smelled nice when all these people came down. But there was only so much time and, oh, the joy of letting go and giving an arrogant son-of-a-bitch—just letting it all fly and giving some jerk just a whale of a—oh God, just one good punch.

The Emigrant

ON HIS WAY TO Kathmandu, Tim Mertz told the woman sitting beside him, "I don't think it's serious."

Her head was in her hands, and she was bent forward.

They were making an emergency landing on Guam, the plane like a cocktail shaker, someone screaming in back, the flight attendants belted into their jump seats. Squeezing his eyes shut as they hit the runway, Tim fought to keep his stomach under control. In the heavy humidity of Guam, they were marched onto a smaller plane that lifted them into a new storm that had blown up behind the storm they'd escaped by landing on Guam. During the failed attempt at a meal service, Tim reached for the hand of the woman, now across the aisle. She was struggling to breathe. He wanted to offer comfort. The woman's grip nearly broke his wrist.

In Bangkok, he boarded a connecting flight, a large jet that seemed suspended from the heavens by a loose elastic. Sitting around him was a group of young men, garrulous, an energy about them suggesting an upcoming athletic challenge. Tim couldn't tell what language they were speaking. Hours later he saw mountains below his window, and then the plane went into clouds. Finally, they descended.

When he stumbled down the long staircase and onto land, his relief was so great he couldn't feel his knees. None of his checked bags had made it. On his way through customs, he realized he'd lost his cell phone. They passed him through. He wandered out a door. An exit.

His sons! Andy and Barry, Andy so much taller than his brother. And Barry—Barry had grown a mustache! Tim hurried to embrace them. For a few moments, he wouldn't let go.

"How was the flight?"

"Eventful!" he said, wanting to sound game and nearly shouting. "But I'm here intact."

"Is that all you brought?"

"Possibly," he laughed, letting Andy take his carry-on. "The other bags took off somewhere. They might turn up."

He saw the boys exchange a look. This was a new and most easygoing father. But then, they didn't know. In the complicated city that was his life, the government had fled, and his streets ran riot. What he'd told the boys before booking this trip was that there'd been hardly enough time to visit with them during their mother's funeral. He wanted to see them. That was all. The fact that his life had come unmoored and he desperately needed an anchor—his sons, family—didn't need saying.

A clear day and those big peaks were? Oh. There. My God. That far away and the size! He asked Barry, "Did you ever trek? That's what you came over for initially, right?"

They had traveled during a college break. Tim had encouraged them. But early the morning after they'd arrived, out for a quick run, they noticed what seemed to be sleeping dogs but were three little boys huddled under a ripped blanket. Tim had heard this story when

Barry called home to tell him they'd cancelled their return flight. Now twenty-one (Andy) and twenty-three (Barry), they ran an orphanage. He recognized the old khakis and windbreakers they were wearing and felt the bittersweet love of a parent whose children were successful at giving rather than getting.

"We were up into elevation areas where the earthquake hit," Barry told him. "It's really beautiful country. But, no, we never did an actual trek."

Andy told him it was turning into a bucket-list item. "See Everest and die. So there's probably time."

"And frankly," Barry said, "it's gotten too crowded."

Tim climbed into the passenger seat of a rusted van, Andy holding the door. As Barry settled behind the wheel, Andy ducked into the back and clubbed a hand over his father's shoulder. Tim grabbed it. Held on a moment.

They gave him a tour of the city, the traffic swift and Tim flinching at the bikes speeding past, everything accelerating, even on the wide boulevard around the palace, the palace itself futuristic and its neighboring architecture not quite what he'd seen in pictures of Beijing or New Delhi.

"I've never seen anything like this," he said. "I should have come out to visit you before this."

"Mom did."

He kept a lighthearted tone in his voice. He wouldn't tell them he'd refused to go with her, refused to even hear about Nepal, because of how hurt and angry he'd been when they'd decided to drop out of college and stay so far from home. Instead, he complained of his workaholic nature, so foolish. "I'll never forgive myself."

"But you finally made it, so it's all good," Andy told him.

"How long are you staying?" Barry asked.

"I'm kind of open ended."

"We're not trying to get you to leave," Barry laughed.

"No," Andy said. "Stay."

Yes. Stay. That was his plan. He was looking up at the buildings that caught his attention. What was particular to Nepal engaged him—the writing like circuitry wire. That singular eye! He needed to like this place.

They left the boulevard and the city center and drove past flanks of apartment buildings before turning down side roads, driving for a long time on narrow streets that were bright-bannered and tossed-looking. They stopped, finally, in front of a large square house, the second and third floors like big blocks plopped onto the first.

It was spare inside. An elderly couple emerged from the kitchen at the back of the house, gray-haired, happy to meet him, an impenetrable Indian accent, their name misheard by him as Magic. Mr. Magic was in a three-piece suit, his wife in a sari of an erotic shade of red.

"How was your flight?"

"Eventful. But I'm here intact!"

Mrs. Magic, staring up at him, touched her chin to indicate his scar.

"Oh. Right," he laughed. "I took it on the chin!" But she missed the joke.

A joke was what he'd wanted. A joke would allow him to forget what had happened. He'd collapsed. After his wife's sudden death, after the funeral, after the boys had flown back to Nepal, his house emptied of friends and family, he'd returned to his law firm strangely agitated. He'd been in trial on a case involving computer coding, the coding rolling on with its font and its crotchets, rolling infinitely on as he chased down among the colons and semicolons, the brackets and commands, the evidence of a copyright infringement. Tim was a talker, a man with no end of stories who digressed, who could paint verbal pictures. When he tried to understand code, the effort made him feel like a man being walked by his dog.

One day in his firm's conference room, he had started babbling, raving on in gibberish, though he'd believed he sounded rational. Thinking he was rational, he went on at length. Where were the words he'd always had to tell the truth? He couldn't find them and began throwing things around—a file, a container of coffee—without being aware of this. Someone made a crack about speaking in tongues just before he fell, catching his chin on the edge of the table. He was stitched up in the ER and kept under observation in the neurology wing, where a cachepot holding a philodendron arrived with a get-well card from his partners and from which he was discharged into his sister's care.

Franny moved Tim into her house, settling him into her guest room after she'd stripped it of anything sharp. For two weeks, he rested in a temporary funk, *temporary* being the operative word as far as he was concerned and *funk* the only medical term to which he'd respond.

"It's terrifying," she told anyone calling about him. "His mind is gone."

One morning, the gloom lifted. Recovered, he marveled at the sound of the birds in the yard.

"I wouldn't put too much stock in birds," Franny told him.

He had to uncover where she'd hidden his wallet, his phone, his shoes, his belt, fleeing like a felon breaking out of prison, over her stone garden wall and through the gate at the end of her driveway.

Back in his own house, he found the furnace had quit. His pipes had frozen, and there was a waterfall in the kitchen. He spent a few days getting repairmen in.

Finally, he went back to work. The building housing his firm was only a three-mile commute, a pleasant drive through suburban streets overhung with chestnut trees. The familiarity was comforting, his parking space like an old slipper. His habit of checking the clock in the lobby returned without bidding. Rejuvenated, he was surprised at the energy he felt. He'd alerted his partners. Would there not be hosannas? Tim is back! Thank God!

He waved to the security guard in the paneled lobby and took the elevator to six. As the door slid open, he found a group of his colleagues waiting.

"I'm back!" Tim greeted them in a louder voice than he'd intended. In an instant, he felt the atmosphere freeze. What?

Lazarus saw faces like these.

They were on their way to court. Hey and hello and how's it going as they bustled past him into the elevator.

He'd hollered, "It's going excellent. Right."

His secretary was in Peru on vacation. There were no files on his desk.

Short of being a comfort, the day oppressed him. The next day was no better. The end of the week brought little relief. Everyone had become hyperfriendly. Everyone spoke as though English were his second language. Everyone was busy. I'm recovered, he'd wanted to shout. But shouting would make things worse.

He began acting the part of a serious and steady man. Very serious. Reliably steady. Anyone coming toward him at an unguarded moment would find him exactly the same as he was every minute of the day: deliberate, sober, mindful.

This became exhausting.

His clients wouldn't take his calls. His clients had been parceled off among his partners. It appeared he wouldn't get any of those clients back. It appeared he no longer had work. He gleaned this sooner than he would have liked. There was a silence around him like a pressure bandage. He went out to lunch with a friend.

"I'm afraid they think I'm crazy. Everyone seems afraid of me."

The friend brushed this aside. "You shouldn't care what people think," he said, but kept an eye on Tim's hand as though he'd snatch up a knife and spring across the table.

He gave himself four months and then recalculated it to six, but things didn't improve. He couldn't live like that. He had to get out of there. After packing his suitcases, he asked a realtor to sell his house and everything in it.

Andy led him upstairs, ushering him into a small bedroom at the back of the second floor. "This has its own bathroom, Dad. And we think it's the quietest."

"Great," he said with cheer. "Very nice."

"You might want a nap," Barry said.

"A nap? No." Before taking off on this trip, he'd imagined himself in their living room, imagined their living room with peaked and inlaid furniture, potted palms, the two boys leaning toward him, listening as he entertained them with a lot of remember-when's. "I just need a moment."

"Are you okay?"

"I'm perfectly fine. Glad to be here."

"We'll let you settle in."

The boys went back downstairs.

He had traveled before, but to hotels, a presence of staff, a schedule. There was a drip noise coming from his bathroom that he wasn't ready to investigate. The walls were white, the thin carpet gray. This was his room then. He took in the low dresser missing a pull and the single bed. No night table. There was a square window and from it, he looked out on a jumble of rooftops. Below was a small yard in which six children played. A woman stood among them, her head bent to them, the gestures of her long brown fingers lovely to his eye. Very beautiful people. He considered the woman, wondered what she might be like. The back wall defining the yard was brick and looked older than the housing around it. This would be his view.

He turned to the bed. His hand pressing the mattress kept going as though the thing would swallow him up. My God, how will I sleep here? From the bag that made the trip in with him—would the others ever be found? Would he even need the good suits that were traveling the world without him?—he pulled out his toiletry kit. In the frigid, off-scented air of the bathroom, he cleaned up quickly and went back downstairs.

With a flourish, he hailed the children sitting along both sides of the long table. Smiles? Some laughter? They stared back at him. Nothing. They have no idea what I'm saying.

He was encouraged into the living room. A series of framed pictures were on the wall. He got up to give them a closer look. Two boys about eight and six years old with what would be cardboard swords. Andy and Barry. For God's sake. In the background, he recognized the large pillars at the front of their house. Well, what do you know. Laughing Barry and wide-eyed, watch-me-quick Andy. They were pretend sword-fighting. Weren't they something at that age. He read his wife's name in the corner. The phantom limb of her absence made him breathless.

From the other room came voices in the local language, and Tim turned his head this way and that as though he'd understand if it came in through something besides an ear. The children's singsong over a scraping of chairs. Happy sounds. How long before they'd leave and his sons could spend some time with him? He sat down again and looked around for a magazine. There were none.

He must have dozed off. Dinner was offered to him as he jumped, startled.

"How was your flight?" the woman he'd seen in the yard asked him. She was older than he'd thought, now he saw her up close. "Was it a very long journey?" She was British. Her English was cockney, the sitar of Nepalese replaced with cracking walnuts.

It took him a moment to realize he could understand what she said. "Eventful. But I'm here intact!" He missed her name, his mind marveling at how she ended up here.

"What a surprise to hear you were on your way to us!" she said. "Your sons were like, 'Dad is arriving to*morrow*! Oh my *God*! He's on his way al*ready*! What'll we *do*?'" With a screaming laugh, she turned and went outside, where the children had gone after their meal.

Tim was then introduced to an older Nepali man, thick-bodied, with a cool composure, called Mr. Soon-as-you're-gone, or a name very similar.

He took the seat directly across from Tim, asking, "How was your flight?"

Tim said, "Eventful! But I'm here intact."

The Magics sat beside Soon-as-you're-gone.

Tim couldn't think of anything he wanted to ask them.

There were candles in shallow dishes on the table. Barry brought out a book of matches and began lighting them.

"Well, well," Tim said with pleasure, tickled by the gesture of celebration.

The food wasn't frightening. He liked to feel adventurous and, anyway, identified rice. Tucking into one of the bowls he'd been served, he found his meal a little dull until he forked up something that felt gelatinous and swallowed it down quickly. The lights flickered and then went out completely.

Andy told Tim the lights would be back on "at some point."

"You light candles every night?" Tim asked.

"Have to," Barry said.

"Who is responsible?" Mr. Magic asked rhetorically. The candlelight glowed in his eyes. "Rolling blackouts in this day and age."

"Our government, if you want to call it a government," Soon-as-you're-gone said to Tim. "Lucky America."

Mr. Magic said, "We follow all your news."

"Primaries and secondaries," Mrs. Magic laughed, but Tim missed this joke if it was one.

Andy ladled more rice onto his dish, and Tim asked him about the sketches in the living room. "Those pictures of you. They were taped to a wall in the kitchen one year."

"That was the summer Mom had us memorizing the St. Crispin's Day speech," Barry said. "She made the swords from poster board. We had a ball."

"'We few! We happy few!'" Andy called, indicating the group at the table.

Mr. Soon-as-you're-gone asked, "This is . . . ?"

"Shakespeare," Barry said.

The name didn't seem to ring a bell.

Andy said, "We had this long, curved staircase in our house, and we used to slide down, paper swords swinging. Or we'd come out from behind the pillars. She sketched us."

"A beautiful likeness," Mrs. Magic said.

"She brought them out with her when she came to see us," Barry said. "It was a surprise."

"So heartbreaking that she's gone."

"Thank you," Andy said.

Mrs. Magic looked at Tim with new eyes. "Curved staircase? This is your home?"

"Yes." His chest hurt, and something angry was in him. He informed the Magics, "Three stories, sunroom across the back, a front porch with pillars. You see in the sketches."

"In the West, you have good builders, though," Mr. Magic said. "It's required." He began to speak generally about housing in a variety of countries, which ended up "crumbling. No requirements."

Tim said, "That house was built more than a century ago. The wood in the floors was a very tight grain. You can't find that now for any price. These days, they harvest wood too quickly. Beamed ceilings, deep moldings. It was put up when they really did things right, really fine work." What was wrong with the food here? he wondered. Something was stuck in his throat. His house. It had needed maintenance. The maintenance, regular as the seasons, had been all he saw in the place. From this distance, with the loveliness of the candlelight, he saw the old white house for what it truly was. "Beautiful. A work of art when you think of it."

"My point entirely. Thank you. Americans are house proud."

"Not me." Tim chuckled. "I'm house-less! It's being sold."

"You're selling our house?" That was Andy.

Barry was staring at him.

"Well. Yes. Maybe you didn't know how much work, I mean, the upkeep on that place. It was constant."

He saw both his sons frown.

Questions were being formed, he was certain. Why hadn't they been asked? Where was he going to live? "I was alone in the place," Tim said quickly. He became afraid then that he would be alone no matter where he ended up.

Mrs. Magic said, "You miss your wife, of course."

He nodded.

Respecting his sentiments, they changed the subject. There was talk about the following day. It seemed they would be going out into the country. The children they found tended to have a parent, a grandparent, sometimes an entire extended family, and the operation was more of a rescue mission, returning trafficked children as well as offering medical help to the families. The Magics were doctors; Tim had missed that during the introduction. They volunteered their skills and would be leaving Nepal in two days. Mr. Soon-as-you're-gone drove one of the vans, or they'd never find their way. Andy was the contact between the children and the families. Barry documented everything for the government. The vans were already overloaded, but Tim was welcome to come. They could squeeze. Really.

"Absolutely not," he laughed. "Don't worry at all about me."

He was sure to find some sightseeing until they were back—though once back, they'd be preparing for some medical people coming in from Switzerland.

"I see," Tim said.

A month later there'd be doctors and nurses from Australia.

Barry said, "We cooperate with other nonprofits, so there's a lot of administration and general getting patients lined up, that sort of thing."

The face of Mr. Soon-as-you're-gone turned slowly in Tim's direction but didn't smile. I'm taking up time better given to children, Tim thought. They don't know me here. No one had asked him to come. Why should they care for him, for what he'd accomplished, what he regretted, the way he loved—all the what-happened and the what-happened next—the whole honeycomb of his life. The children were far more important, obviously. A door at the back of the dining room had "Office" printed on it, and the door was closed. What would he do here? How would he be useful? He could take his money out, but time with the boys was the reason he'd come. When he turned to them, he saw the pain of losing their mother and now the home that connected them to her. Would anyone in this room care that he'd moved here to save his life? The lights bounced back on, and he had to keep from shouting at the surprise of it.

The group around him began to stir. Barry got up and walked into the kitchen. Tim watched his son's back moving away from him and felt a slight panic.

Mr. Magic asked him, "You have more bags coming? Is that what I heard?"

He would check on them tomorrow, he said, his tone upbeat, brave. The idea of getting himself around and collecting the missing luggage appeared to him as an impossible challenge, an Everest. He wanted to say this out loud. He wanted to howl, to make himself known.

Andy cleared the plates off the table. The children's voices sang in the yard. For a long time, the Magics talked with Soon-as-you're-gone, deciding something. Tim heard them without listening. He would adjust, he told himself. He would learn the customs and some words and a way to get around. Wasn't that what people did?

Mr. Soon-as-you're-gone leaned toward him, asking, "You agree?"

The Magics were waiting for his response.

What? What am I agreeing to? His lost house and the early years of his life were setting up camp in the front of his mind. He'd no idea what had just been said. Bound to their mercy, he agreed.

The Flying Boat

IN 1921, VERA CONOR, on her way home from work, saw her brother Dan waiting under the glass-and-iron awning of a tea shop and felt his sunny disposition dispel the gloom of an overcast London day. He was a big, broad-shouldered man, hard to miss. And someone was with him. Vera would remember the moment she first set eyes on Neil Leahy, who was dangerous-looking even in civilian clothes.

"Neil is a language teacher," Dan told her.

She gave her brother a sidelong glance that he wouldn't respond to. "What language?" she asked Neil.

"All a them," he said and leveled a look at her.

She fell in love with him. It was the way he was looking at her, the way he stood, the way he simply was. In love, she lost track of time and place.

Her brother said, "Tea and a bit of bread, Vera, love? We've had uncontrollable costs. We're out the biscuit money."

She led them into the tea shop, which was empty of customers. The two men sat with their backs to the wall. The shop owner came out, and Vera ordered for them. When the woman left, she regarded the satchel her brother had tucked against his leg and understood what they were carrying home. As the Irish war for independence battled into its fifth Easter, Ireland was running out of bullets.

Had they enough money for a meal, she might never have met Neil Leahy. The chance of their meeting was that slim. And so her mind began racing.

"I work for the post office," she said. "Here in London. Give me the stuff, and I'll post it home to Mum."

"Too dangerous," Dan said very softly.

But she saw Neil watching her, felt his estimate of her move where she wanted it. Staring right back at him, she said, "They look for fellows like you two. They don't look for a pretty girl."

It was like her to call herself pretty. She believed in the power of suggestion and wanted everyone to think she had a lot of nerve. Slim, a clotheshorse, well able to wrap and post a package out of sight of her housemates, she was twenty-one, the same age as the century and eager to get on with things. Her convent school was well behind her. Where was adventure?

The tea came on a tray, and she poured for them. Clearly, they were hungry. Neil wolfing down sandwiches gave Vera a good idea of what kind of place he'd come from.

She told them, "I posted a box home to Mum only a fortnight ago. Some dishes. She loves getting packages from me."

When they'd finished, they got up from the table with Vera holding the satchel.

He came back, the supposed language teacher, alone and happy to see her. They walked around the neighborhood like a couple only interested

in each other and perhaps the birds or the tops of the trees. He handed
over a cloth sack holding a wooden box, sealed shut and heavy.

"You like London?" he asked her.

"I love it," she told him. "I have friends here."

He considered this. "I've nothing against your average fella."

"I want Ireland free," she told him. "I do want that."

"Well good luck to us, then. I wasn't sure you'd want to send more
mail."

"I think I'm very good at it."

"Aye," he laughed. "You truly are."

She tried not to keep looking over at him. The point was to look
ordinary, and she had trouble with the ordinary part of it since she
was over the moon.

She mailed boxes to her mother again and again, some very large and
difficult to carry, finally catching the notice of her supervisor, who told
her she was about the most devoted daughter he'd ever known. Many
times, she thought her heart was trying to beat itself out of her breast.
She was so afraid something in the shape of the box or the butcher paper
and heavy string—something rattling, God forbid—might signal what
she was up to. She could be hanged.

Meetings with Neil were brief. Sooner or later, they'd end. To win him,
finally, she traveled home to Roscommon that summer and asked Dan
to bring him around. They came by on the third night of her holiday.
She watched him take in the size of the rooms, the velvet curtains,
the rugs and the chandelier. There was a spread of dinner steaming in
serving bowls on the wide table and bottles lined along the sideboard.
She'd been right to suspect Neil had come from a rough place. His effort
at looking unimpressed was almost successful.

The younger kids still home—Michael and Dennis—were awestruck
by him. They wanted his opinions and advice. They asked for stories.
The children of Vera's eldest sister, Deirdre, who lived nearby, ran in.
(Deirdre stayed home. Deirdre, a martyr, disapproved of Vera going to

London alone for a job.) It was a boisterous crowd made louder by her mother's revolutionary opinions.

By evening's end, Neil was telling them a story from his childhood (something to do with a carton of books, but in the details, Vera realized he might have lacked parents and even a bed to sleep in), laughing loudly, complimenting Vera's mother for her politics in the most florid speech, kidding Michael and Dennis, who were still beaming admiration for him. When he had to leave, it was obvious he didn't want to go. He gave Vera a look she had no trouble translating.

He wrote to her. She realized that, despite his background, he'd managed to get an education. *My Dearest Vera* . . . and she began to feel the spell he described himself under. One letter that stood out from the seductive ones confessed to her how he'd felt the first day they'd met.

> *We three like another trio of musketeers. I thought at the time of the three legs of one stool where you only had strength because of each other. I'll belabor the metaphor, won't I? But I wanted you to see how you could rely on me and that the cause made me what I was. The cause and the times are all very tremendous to me and you became part of that. It's the soul that understands. I know the poets say this better, but it's to your soul I am bound.*

Months later, he slipped out of Ireland, having heard that his death was being arranged and, unable to wait for American immigration, sailed to Argentina. *My Dearest Vera.* . . . He found a job teaching. He taught languages in a private school for the children of wealthy expats. A language teacher after all. She had a good laugh at that. *My most darling Vera.* . . . She followed him to Buenos Aires. The steamer was too slow, too full of languid passengers. In one of her bags was her wedding dress.

How was she to keep from loving Buenos Aires? The city was European. But it wasn't really. Her homesickness overwhelmed any affection she might feel for her new country. BA would work its magic on her, Neil said, but it was Neil who had her entranced.

During the early years, with the birth of their two sons, the Leahys made friends with the Caseys, also from Ireland, and through the Caseys came friendship with the Kellys, both lawyers. The Caseys and Kellys brought them together with Delia and Tony Murphy. In the way friends orbit around one another, Delia, so effusive, and Tony, so hospitable, tended to be the center. It was a close little group, English-speaking.

"Sympatico," Delia said. "How is it we all get along so well?"

Vera thought their cohesiveness came from a lack of competition; she was the adventuresome one, something of a war hero in her mind, the risk-taker, as opposed to the softhearted one (Mercedes Kelly) or the intellectual (Maria Casey) or the theatrical Delia.

"The point," Vera said one night when they were all together, "is to save up and have our stake and go back to Ireland with it. Have our pick of a place and settle down."

"You'll never leave Argentina. It's too congenial."

The elder of Neal and Vera's two sons came into the dining room, eleven years old and getting very tall that year. Something of her brother Dan, of her family's look, was on him, and she grinned seeing him. He stayed only a moment because, with Delia Murphy there, they'd be arguing politics.

"A peaceful discussion," Delia Murphy insisted, "I promise. I don't like arguments. Only good feelings."

But then Delia would go on and on about the recent military junta, and there was the Depression crippling her beloved country. The problem, Delia cried, was the loss of Argentina as a world power. "We were there. We were just about to take the world stage. And Vera wants to leave."

Neil laughed, telling her not to worry since any move back to Ireland depended on having enough savings. "Our ship hasn't come in."

In 1933 the owners of the school left for England, leaving Neil in charge. He worked out of his own small office, avoiding the bigger vacated ones. In time, those abandoned rooms grew eerie looking. The owners never returned. Soon, the school went up for sale, and Neil told Vera the new buyers would surely keep him on.

"How much is it going for?"

When he told her the amount, he added, "But they're sure to find someone to take it over, even at that price."

"It's us," Vera told him. "We're going to be the buyers."

"Vera, it's too much."

He was still in love with her. She saw it in his eyes after she said that. She was game, the adventurous one, a woman who could make things happen. He was right that they couldn't afford it. A wedding cake of a mansion, it had been converted into classrooms at the turn of the century by a navy man. Instilled with the fear of scurvy, he'd covered its acre of ground with orange trees.

"I'm only employed there," Neil said. "The new owners will take care of us."

"What if they don't? They could dismiss you. And you know how to run the place. You're already doing it. I'll help you."

"A mortgage to cover the price, do you have any idea—"

"What did you do all that fighting for independence for? Ireland is free, but you're not. The new headmaster could be someone you can't stand. You'll be waiting for what falls from his table. If he keeps you on. This is our opportunity."

When she'd finally convinced him, she put together the paperwork to secure a mortgage, and they moved in. They hired teachers and paid the monthly interest on their loan, knowing the full amount was out there and could crush them if they didn't make a success. It was another war, she realized. A financial war of survival, but war nonetheless. Alive to it, she was tireless. She helmed the administration duties and contacted the parishes around the city for more people who might send their children to the school. There was upkeep. There were receptions where they'd meet people in government, people with school-age children. Neil was a fine teacher, but she was the one to manage a staff, a director who kept doing a chore even after others joined in. Nothing was beneath her. During the summer break, to help their income, she and the boys picked the oranges on the school grounds and sold them.

The movement forward was so incremental, so full of different elements, it took a scene in Neil's office to make her realize they'd come through all right. Neil was with the Polish consul and his wife, the three of them apparently having just shared a joke. That would be Neil making them comfortable. She had coffee brought in. Neil's suit made him seem an old world *professore*, she thought, noticing how well turned out her husband looked. His hair was thinning, and there was that expression of contentment he wore lately. She took a quick measure of the consul's wife. The couple was enrolling their sons in the school. Not the first of the diplomat population—and not the first time Vera thought of building additional classrooms. It was 1938, she had left the selling of oranges behind, but she was only now recognizing how far behind.

The consul's sons could start midway through the semester, Neil told her later. "They're advanced, the two of them. They may be ahead of their classes."

"I don't know where we'll put them," she said. When he laughed at that, she said, "It's better than wealth, isn't it?" meaning the particular life they had. She looked over at him, certain he shared her thinking.

"What is?" he asked. "A consulate?"

"No. Us. We'll see the consul and his wife socially now and then. They're interesting." Vera had just received a letter from her sister Deirdre that was dull with complaints. "Imagine only seeing people who wore you down. And money isn't any guarantee they'll be interesting."

"The consul isn't wealthy," Neil said. "I know they're having a time of it making the tuition."

She started laughing. "That isn't what I meant."

"What is?" He was cross.

Still laughing, she said, "Never mind!" She gave up.

Furious, he said, "I can make room for their sons!"

"Good," she said, angry at him now. What was wrong with him?

. . .

It was some months later, when they were on their way to a dinner party at the Murphys' house, that Vera felt a change in her emotional atmosphere. Something was slightly off. She sensed herself in some kind of trouble, and the insecurity this gave her was immediate.

Delia Murphy, who generally welcomed Vera with a quick acknowledgement, held her arm with both hands. "Vera, how beautiful you look." She seemed to be waiting for Vera to give her an answer to something. Well, Delia was all drama. And Delia always kissed Neil hello as though the sight of him aroused her unmercifully. Tonight, she avoided looking at him.

When they were seated at the table, Vera tried to catch Neil's eye because she'd grown even more ill at ease.

Neil was saying, "It's an anniversary today. Of the day I decided to buy the school . . ."

Vera heard this distinctly. He was across from her but at the opposite end of the table, and his head was turned toward Maria Casey. Vera found Mercedes Kelly focused intensely on her and saying with a gush of empathy something about how lovely Vera's new eyeglasses were.

"Well I don't know about that," Vera said. But the story of how she realized she needed eyeglasses was comical. Leaning forward to tell her friend what happened, she was stopped by the certainty that, if she began some entertaining anecdote, she would be making a fool of herself.

Neil was saying, "If I waited to see what the new owner was like, it would be too late. So the obvious turn was to risk it . . . buy the school myself."

She stared at Neil. It was impossible to see in him the rough freedom fighter with whom she'd fallen into bed moments after she'd arrived here, her traveling suit only half off, the window shutters still open. He was so altered, she thought. He shared *abrazos* and loved *matambre arrollado* at his favorite *bodegon*. He bought the Spanish newspaper every day at the local kiosk. *A porteños*. Was he even Irish at all anymore? He loves it here.

He was *in* love. She realized there was a question floating amid the scent of lilies from one of her dinner companions to the other: Does Vera know?

Delia. Of course. And Delia would not be like the others. The others were suspicions, well founded, that hurt her (and what life has no hurt in it? she'd asked herself before getting on with things and ignoring her husband's foolishness), but the others never made landfall on Neil and Vera's marriage. Delia would want to make a scene. However things played out wouldn't matter to Delia, only the circus it inspired, with Delia very much the center. Vera turned to get some assessment of Tony Murphy and realized he was pleasantly drunk. Tony wouldn't have to figure out the new part he'd been given. But Vera felt her character being twisted into the role of victim, a role she couldn't play. It would be poor Vera from now on. The apologetic look of concern from Mercedes Kelly made her physically ill. She felt her soul being murdered.

Before the night ended, Delia hurried over to her, took her hands in hers, and said something (Vera was too upset to listen) "Glad . . . !" "How wonderful you . . . ," or perhaps it was, "Oh my dear Vera . . . " the sort of brush full of glue to smack across her mouth, *Don't say a word. Behave so I can have my fun.* Her little audience of friends *would* stay intact, yes?

As Vera Leahy stepped down into the airplane, shifting her weight to keep her balance, a hand shot out and grabbed hers, helping her forward.

"Well done." She laughed, turning to a uniformed American, a man she felt was stronger than her entry needed. "Are you in charge here?" but he had already turned to a couple boarding just behind her.

She moved into the lounge. There were a handful of other passengers causing the plane to bob and list slightly. She smiled at them, thinking they were a good omen; Neil had told her no one was crazy enough to get on the thing.

"Oh, I'm going," she'd told him.

He said very seriously, "It couldn't be helped."

"Really," she'd said.

He told her, "I'll not be made the bad guy."

For a moment, she almost stayed. There was a temptation to battle his rendition of what happened, do whatever it would take to win the fight of who would be manager of the truth of it.

It was cozy, she found, the main cabin with the look of a smoking lounge, bright-blue seats, the windows closed against a frigid morning, the wide river winking back at her. The man who'd helped her on board now guided her through the plane to show her where her berth was, and she tossed her overnight bag with her cotton suit (it would be spring on the other side of the equator) onto the bed before going back to sit and have a cigarette.

An eager-looking group sat around her, though no one she cared to chat up, she was still so furious.

"Nervous?" asked the man sitting across from her.

"Not a bit," she snapped.

Turning his attention to his seat belt, "Right," he said barely audibly and belted himself in.

She watched him and followed suit, realizing the steward was close enough to touch and saying all manner of welcomes and information. I am losing my mind, she thought and decided this was hilarious. Moments later, the pilot and navigator having gone up to the cockpit, the plane shuddered to life. Dear God, she thought. And indeed, Mary and Joseph as well. But she felt pleased with herself: she was on an airplane—a flying boat to be exact—taxiing endlessly up and down the river.

Why is it doing this, she wondered. "Are we fishing?" she asked the man she'd been rude to, but he wouldn't look at her.

Finally, some feverish engine noise, and they began racing and then peeling up from the river that was blistering around them. They bounced down into the water again and pulled up. Spray pummeled like a rainstorm against the bottom of the plane as they continued, faster, lifting again and touching down again until finally shedding the earth and trying their luck with the bruising air. Neither fish nor fowl, she thought. She was terrified. This was fun.

The flight was from Buenos Aires to New York, where she'd get on the plane to Foynes, Ireland. In Ireland, she'd be met by her brother Dan. Dan would drive her home to her mother, and her mother would listen to her pour out her heart.

In Vera's mind, her mother would say, "Of course you can stay and begin a divorce. I may be Roman Catholic, but I'm your mother first and foremost." And when Vera writhed in guilt and sorrow, her mother would say, "Your two boys are grown up. They're getting ready for college. They speak Spanish, Vera, love. They don't understand half of what you say anyway."

The steward brought her a whiskey. The plane with its endless drone struggled through the air, like someone having trouble getting to sleep. She joined the other passengers taking their plates into the cabin, where a buffet had been arranged, platters of sliced steak, empanadas, and stuffed tomatoes. The talk was animated and about Germany and Hitler, talk that would continue when she took her seat at the table.

"He won't...."

"Well, he wouldn't...."

"It's the land of Goethe, for God's sake. And Bach! They're poets. What's come over them?"

She looked out the window and found she was looking down along the spine of a passing bird.

It was the absence of war talk that struck her on the flight from New York to Ireland, that and a new group of passengers, all of them men. She found them competing to charm her and understood this was only a contest among themselves. Vera happily played her part in this—a good way to kill time, for they'd be more than a day flying over the Atlantic. American news. American business. She gradually became aware of the lone holdout; here was someone very alert and very recognizable to her, carrying something across a border, she was certain, for she spotted a soft briefcase resting like a good dog against his leg. She would have loved to wink at him, do something to claim a kindred soul. You're good, she thought of him. You're surely on about something.

After a night's sleep, she found they were only an hour from landing. The conversation in the dining room was muted. They were racing toward Europe, and the war was now very close. How peaceful it looks, she thought, seeing the cliffs along the edge of Ireland. The plane descended and then roared up the River Shannon, giving her the sensation they were traveling much faster now. Were they going all the way to Roscommon?

A town was to their right. The water came up close to them, and the pontoons under the wings thunked slightly and bobbed up and down. The engines were turned off, and men on the ground pulled the aircraft to shore with ropes. When one of them noticed her face in the window, she opened the curtains wider. An Irish face. She waved. He waved back.

After customs, she looked for Dan and caught sight of—yes, because he turned, it was Dan, though she might not have recognized him. He'd lost a great deal of weight. A shrunken, ordinary-looking man. The sight of him shocked her.

"Oh," she cried and held a hand high in greeting. "Dan! It's me!"

Even his walk was different, hesitant, a limp. "Welcome home." He gave her a quick hug. "Look at yourself," he said with admiration. "Still the girl of the hour."

She felt her past roaring back to her, the energy of her youth.

"Have you much baggage?"

"Only this," she said, pointing to a suitcase and the overnight bag.

"You've made a good job of it. You've not changed, Veer."

They hurried through the wide room and out to the fresh air.

He told her, "They've scared up a bit of dinner for you up home. Should be a good meal you're in for."

"Good, good." She felt breathless. "And how are you doing?"

He laughed. "Compared to what?"

She glanced over at him, recalling his younger self when he "ran the shop," as Neil put it.

"I'm ticking over," he told her. "I keep busy with the odd jobs."

"Another dog?" she joked of his car.

"Aye," he said. "Another one that keeps playing dead."

They drove from the car park and east along the Shannon.

Before she could ask what he was doing lately, he said, "I'm on my way to America. In a week, if you don't mind. Michael and Dennis said to come."

She remembered the boyhood faces on their two younger brothers and found herself grinning. They were in Boston. "For construction work?"

"They could set me up bartending. That's the hope. I'm a bit off balance for the building trades."

"They'd love to see you," she said.

"There's nothing here for me, and I can use the company."

"You wouldn't go to Argentina?" she asked grimly.

"Your end of town? And do what? Work for Neil? He was under my command. I used to give him orders."

She felt the little car accelerating.

Dan asked, "How is your man at all?"

"You wouldn't know him."

"Is that right?"

"Neil is no longer Neil. I'm telling you, even his language is all new. You wouldn't recognize him on the street."

"Go 'way."

"And he's prosperous."

"Well, we know that would be thanks to yourself, don't we?" he said. "Cornelius Leahy was up for anything, good man, but you had to tell him what it was."

She brought out her cigarettes. Her hands shook, and she waited a moment before giving one to him.

"Thanks then."

"How is Mummy?"

"In and out of the world as we know it. Deirdre and her kids are over there with her. She's too unsteady on her own. The memory escapes her."

The view from her window was relentless, the cloud cover so dense and gray she realized how used to the sunny skies of Argentina she'd become. "Things don't sound too good."

"Ah, we'll keep the tone up while you're about. We won't let you see the dreary."

"When did Deirdre move home?"

"You two are chalk and cheese, aren't you! She's not moved in so much as she's over there the better part of the day. Helping."

"Helping. Good God."

"You can handle Deirdre, Veer. It's only a visit. How long are you home for?"

"Oh," she said as though it was all the same to her. But she was becoming aware of the burden she might be to people who had to "scare up" a meal. She looked out on what seven years of war and then years of the Great Depression had done to the countryside. This was a foreign place to her now and desolate. There would be no work for her, nothing for her to do that wouldn't take the job away from someone already living here. The landscape passed by her and didn't know her. "Not long," she said finally. "I've the boys to get back for. My young men," she laughed. She was trying to sound lighthearted. "And the school, of course."

"You've invested quite a lot into that school."

She felt something hard fill her chest. "No lazing about for me then. A good visit will do, and then off I go."

She would have to go back to Argentina. She didn't want to. What she'd do at her return, she couldn't imagine. So far away, the place seemed like something she'd dreamed. But here, Ireland, was nothing like she remembered. She glanced over at Dan, who was looking balefully over the steering wheel with what was left of him.

"They say there'll be war in Europe," she said, wanting a subject that wasn't Neil.

"They'll have to do it without me."

"But you think it's coming?"

"I do."

"Do you miss the old days?"

"Never," he said. "Don't tell me you do."

"I miss. . . ." Everything, she wanted to say. "I miss being useful, I suppose." Thrilled and on tenterhooks was what she meant. Alive. She missed being alive.

She had been watching the countryside as they drove and began to realize the view was not going to improve—the overgrowth, the abandonment, the cottages that seemed to have gone down on one knee.

"We're off to the shook merchants," he laughed.

"But isn't it all changed?"

"Give us a rest. You sound like Mr. Yeats. Sure it's changed. It's poorer."

The verges and the green fields slipping past, she thought of the man who'd been silent on the flight over, the courier bag.

"I might take a quick trip to London," she said. "I've still got old friends there."

"You could be caught in the war that's on its way to them."

"You think so?"

Her mind raced ahead of the car. She'd see her mother after all this time, see if her mother remembered her. And there'd be her visit with Deirdre to manage. Afterward, she'd travel to her old friends. It would be easy to stay in London and find something that needed her. She would be useful again. Excitement filled her, excitement and love and calm, and she marveled at the road on which rage and refusal had placed her.

"Oh, it's all too much, isn't it," she said, laughing, her voice high.

"I'm inclined to think otherwise," Dan said.

"No, but I'm able for it," she said as though he could read her mind and know her plans and those plans bright-new and only just catching her eye. He wouldn't cheer up, and so she began singing "Down by the Salley Gardens," a song he sang when they were kids. He had a tenor and had taken himself very seriously, hoping for a music career before the world blew up. She sang it now in a quickened tempo, letting her voice jump when the car hit a bump, every verse until she got him to smile.

The Wild Hair

for Brian Kuhn

EVERYONE'S BEEN through this, I imagine, the police at the door.
I was a scientist, so the police appeared to me as all inclusive groups do, puzzles to be considered. And beyond the relief they promised (dealing with the dead body so we didn't have to), there was the comfort of knowing it wasn't my house they were giving such a cool looking over. We were at Rain Wellman's house. Rain had been absent from work. We'd texted. We'd discussed possibilities after a second day of silence. When we drove over to her place on day three, we found her in a scene oddly familiar; we'd witnessed the same pose in a movie that had been released a year earlier. The movie had only been sad. The sight of Rain shook us to our bones.

With no evidence to the contrary, Rain's death was declared a suicide. It had, in fact, looked self-inflicted. But it wasn't suicide. We knew who killed her. We also knew the man—such as he was—would never be found. Yet Aldous and I searched for him. Yesterday, after years of looking, we spotted him, and in the most unlikely of places.

This story begins in Taiwan. No one there on September 21, 1999, will forget the earthquake that caused the entire island to shudder before undulating first one way and then another. It registered 7.3 on the Richter scale. Among the over two thousand deaths was one Dr. Manson Lee, a nuclear physicist living close to the epicenter in Chichi Township. Though his body was recovered from the rubble, his papers were not. He had been living under the assumed name of Han. The subterfuge had been discovered only hours before the earth erupted beneath everyone.

Lee had been the designer and engineer for a launch ten years earlier of a rocket intended for Pluto, a rocket that failed to follow its expected route. With China growing powerful, Taiwan hoped to gain some leverage on the world stage. The rocket missed its slingshot moment and found a wormhole that sent it off in an unplanned direction. It proceeded on what US Intelligence called "a joyride," also calling it in a more private communication, "a physicist's wet dream," for its speed was unprecedented. How the spacecraft was able to travel with such velocity would have been the subject of Lee's papers. But the Taiwanese government disavowed the failed mission, and Lee disappeared—hiding in plain sight as Han. Whoever had tracked him down to take possession of his work arrived too late and was presumed killed by the earthquake. The spaceship was forgotten; once it sped beyond a certain distance, no one could find it and Taiwan, aware of derision, of accusations that the launch had never happened, didn't want to talk about it.

In 2007, Rain and I were working in New Jersey for Aldous Field. From the early days of tech, he'd invested in start-ups and had amassed billions. The size of his fortune separated him from the general population, and even with the number of billionaires extant, he felt alone. I believe this combination of exclusiveness and loneliness was the impetus for his particular fancy. He believed in life in the far reaches of outer space and wanted us to tune in and capture a click or a sigh, anything signifying other beings. His exceptional longing for even the slightest proof that earth had company in this vast "heaventree of stars" was where he put his money.

At this time, the thinking of many scientists was that extraterrestrial intelligent life might be less inclined to use advanced technology to simply say, "Hello, anyone home out there?" They might be more inclined to concentrate on their own particular interplanetary needs. Astrophysicists had begun asking themselves, Why should they bother about us? Might they be in need of new defense systems and types of energy? They might not care about humans on far earth but rather how to gain dominance and survive in their own corner of the universe. We had been assuming the advanced intelligence of beings without wondering if they were even audible, let alone curious about us.

Aldous didn't like this thinking. He had initially tried to work with the SETI Institute in Mountain View, California, but after a fight with the people who ran the place, he took his money to the other side of the country. The result was our own ATA-350 on top of Jenny Jump Mountain. The site, I liked to note, was just beyond an amusement park called the Land of Make Believe.

"Say something!" I'd joke to my computer screen. I'm not sure I ever believed that some chirp would come to us. When I'd entered MIT's engineering school, my intent was a DNA-level cure for Alzheimer's. But the road through medical research became financially daunting. I had debt. Taking over the Field Institute's computer for an impressive paycheck was an easy choice. As my mentor put it, "There's grant money, Molly, of course, but you can't beat a billionaire with a wild hair up his ass."

For a year, I listened. I listened hard to a lot of nothing. Then one afternoon in 2008, just as the markets began to crash, Rain was sitting near me, and I found myself listening to her. Rain loved confiding. I consider sharing confidences proof of the human soul—bring it on. I don't gossip, I might add. We were the senior scientists in the place, and when I'd first started working with her—thrilled that the institute was being run by two women—I showed interest and empathy, even enjoying her stories.

The problem was that Rain had a way of giving too much information, specifically about her complicated sex life. That day, while I worried about my mortgage being underwater, she had an anecdote I'd heard before, an Iliad of a threesome that had ended with a lost wig. I should have enjoyed it for the umpteenth time, and perhaps if she had some conviction about what she was doing, I might have, but I always felt her using me as a gauge to find out if she'd been brave and rebellious and au courant rather than gullible, used, and liable to return to this later as the source of self-destructive behaviors. A few keystrokes and my screen filled with the heavens, dark and in motion. I took my attention onto its shores. Rain talked on, but I was like someone on a beach waving a metal detector first one way and then the other, blissfully hoping to find something of value.

In time, I would have gone back to the programming I was supposed to be doing, but Rain would've known and moved her chair over to assist me. And talk to me. I remained looking at unfamiliar space, advancing beyond the beyond of the Milky Way's blissful silence. We all have memories of troubles and lost chances, and I consoled myself that a need for peace wasn't an insult to my colleague. I wasn't obligated to let her drive me crazy. There, as I studied my screen, came a signal from what I thought was a bit of floating junk. My attention was completely taken by it. Rain, realizing her audience was gone, returned to her own calculations and mapping.

Aldous came into the room, which was always significant since he was six five and sadly clumsy. A street kid from Sydney, Australia, he'd won scholarships to college and a green card to the States, where a talent for picking investments, a genius for it, delivered to him all manner of riches. I loved Aldous for being living proof that money can't buy everything. Few people I've known have been as socially uncomfortable.

He talked to Rain as I worked, asking how close she thought we might be, how soon we might connect.

Was it junk that I'd found? I struggled to unlock its brain. Carefully, I dodged and angled my way forward. Then I let out a yell. I was in. But in what?

"I think it's Mandarin," I said. "It's a kind of Mandarin. Holy shit."

"What?"

"Put it up on the big screen, Molly," Rain said.

"I think it's the Taiwanese."

"What are they doing?"

"They had a launch. Years ago. It was lost."

"You found it?"

"Maybe."

For a long time, we were looking at the equivalent of what you'd see on a CAT scan, something like the wily pancreas maybe. We had nothing but blobby gray and my frustration trying to figure it out.

"Rain," I said. "Find out where I am."

She called out to Ben, who came in from his office and joined us.

Aldous pulled up a chair, sitting with shallow breath and a handkerchief out to mop his face.

It was hard to navigate the system. I worried that the craft was going so fast it wouldn't respond. Finally, I managed to open what I found to be an aperture. Once I opened it, the entire room went silent. On the big screen, the color gray slid up like an eyelid. A view of far outer space, magnificent and heart-stopping, greeted us.

"You're sure this isn't Hubble?"

"Molly," Ben said to me after a few moments, "you're looking at NGC 185."

"That's too far." I felt my breathing go shallow. On the big screen were quasars and superclusters that the spacecraft treated like so many mile posts on a highway. "It's like thousands of light years. The craft was launched in 1989. It can't be that far."

"It is," Rain said.

"How?" Was this the answer to gravitational force in the universe? Where were the black holes to crush this thing? "How," I said again, and I could hear panic in my voice.

Aldous said, "There's more than us. There's someone out there."

But there wasn't. I spent the rest of the day and most of the night watching. The spacecraft was traveling at a stunning rate. We had to keep up with what it saw. We had eyes on new territory, and of course, the word *territory* was incorrect. We had eyes on new space. How the craft achieved its velocity was only one of the puzzles I needed to solve. How and when to let the rest of the world in on our discovery would have to wait while we scrambled to keep up with all we were seeing.

A week later, Rain and I took a break from all the data we were recording and all the questions with which we found ourselves.

"I have nightmares," she said. "I'm trying to imagine what's way out there. I'm afraid of what we'll find. Who. It."

"I don't think it'll find anything," I said. "You saw what was on the screen. Nothing but rocks."

"How do you do it, Molly?"

"That spacecraft is so old. The computer in it is like a toy. Hardly a problem breaking into it."

"No. How do you live so self-contained and content?"

I was anything but content. As for self-contained, that could mean stiff. If anything, I was a seething mess of need. My daily arguments with myself about wasting my talents for a fat paycheck from a man who couldn't be satisfied with a voice from his next-door neighbor was nothing compared to the crush I had on him. One can't fall in love with people like Aldous, I knew. The money gets in the way. No, I hardly thought of myself as content. But I didn't want to admit to anything. Rain thought I was self-contained because that was how I kept from being like her. Even as I shrugged off her description of me, she'd launched into another saga, this time her dysfunctional childhood and the question of whether she should call her mother, extend a hand, open her heart, but for her concerns about her mother's . . . back-and-forth over the abyss of the caveats.

"Rain," I said to change the subject. "Did it cross your mind that this might be staged? That we're watching something put together in Arizona? That it's having us on?"

"Why would anyone do that? For what reason?"

"Because they can?"

"You can't believe it's real?"

"I don't want to."

"Sorry. I can't get my head around that. Arizona. Sometimes I think you could drive me completely over the edge with that kind of thinking."

It was the following day that we saw it. At 13:42 eastern standard time, as we stared up at the beautiful but inert orbs, the writhing labor of star births, the long speeding camera angle on what, for a while, was open space, there came into view what shot us out of our seats, arms high in the air, mouths open. We saw a blue marble veiled in some clouds, sporting a single moon. It was our twin. We screamed. We ended up in tears.

Late that night, I went home to the house I'd bought in Bridgewater. The house, even after the 2008 crash, always comforted me, and my mood that night was very fragile. I went out to the back deck and looked up at what was visible of the night sky. It isn't true that scientists are all atheists. It's more that words can't describe the vastness, the subatomicness, the whole . . . I could never find the words. Religions live on words. But the universe? Even with ambient light, there were enough stars over me to leave me speechless. And now another earth. My soul was reeling.

Momentarily, I have to add, a strange sensation took me. It was as though the house behind me, the deck under my feet, had become electrified. Then the sensation passed. All appeared to be well again.

· · ·

This all seems so long ago, perhaps because of the innocence of those early days.

I found the way to direct the ship and arrested its fierce speed forward. We were able to observe the other earth at leisure. One of my worries had been that the craft had sped around in a circle and that we were simply looking down at our own planet. But no. Florida was missing. Mexico bumped into half the bay. To look down at an unmapped North America, one can visualize an obese ballerina balancing on a toe. Here that inkblot test delivered more of a heavy-shouldered professor, arms akimbo. As our twin turned, Australia's north had a land ladder to China that took in many of our own archipelagoes. Italy, remarkably, still had a boot, but Africa had no horn and was almost double in size, leaving part of the Atlantic more of a channel.

With the topography of the planet looking so serene from our distance, I thought the place a new Eden, a primitive environment. But there was a string of satellites winking around the middle of this big blue sphere like a necklace, so perfectly strung were they. Two hundred by our first count, though we'd continue to count as the sphere turned in its orbit. The regimentation of the satellites was telling, each equidistant from its neighbors.

And then—hallelujahs from Aldous, who began all but dancing around the room—we were able to pick up sound. It was not from our mountaintop ATA-350. I confess I stumbled onto this. I'd been working night and day to improve the picture, wanting a closer look. That was not to happen. I was stuck beyond the planet's atmosphere, unable to accelerate closer. But during this time, I began to hear speech. Or something like speech. The satellites were close enough that we assumed ourselves into a kind of party line. We could hear them. What they were saying was incomprehensible beyond my understanding this was communication among living beings.

"Can you decipher it?" Aldous asked.

"... trying."

"It sounds like grunting," Aldous said.

"So does English to some people."

"But you can figure it out?"

I hoped to. Language has repetitions. But even with all the linguistics in my background, this would be hard.

Before three months had passed, I began to hear speech in English. *Hello. Hello, how are you? I am fine, how are you? Not too bad, great weather we are having. We're having. Remember the conjunctions.*

"Aldous!" I yelled. "Come quick!"

We listened, the entire institute, Aldous using my headphones and weeping, the other scientist, the assistants, the interns, all rapt. Two people were hired to develop a rollout of the Field Institute's findings. Many people had scoffed at Aldous, and now he'd have his vindication.

The conversations from the far end of the heavens grew more complex. One man sounded like an auctioneer for a tobacco-leaf sale. A woman gave a list of questions, like *What time should we arrive? Where is there a car dealership? Is it cash or credit or debit?*

And two months later, when every one of us longed to converse with them, to ask how things went in their world, to have our hopes rewarded with evidence of cooperation and peace, we heard music. Earth music. Frank Sinatra and Judy Garland. Prince. But also a song I had to research to find was "Love Letters Straight from Your Heart" by Timi Yuro, or someone giving a perfect rendition of Timi Yuro. Then rappers. Lizzo and the non-sequitur song. Then Billie Holliday, Beyoncé, and Billy Eckstine. Then the soundtrack from *The Music Man*. Next was Washington's valedictory song from *Hamilton*. I was beginning to get an odd but unnamable sensation.

To say we had many questions was an understatement. Who were they? How had they evolved? Had they exploded the atom? Did they have ten fingers and ten toes? What system of government? Beliefs? Ethics? Energy? Had they global warming? Had they solved it? It was too much to consider all the infinitesimal parts that made our own planet quite what it was at that moment. Were they an identical twin or fraternal? We saw their water, knew there was oxygen, realized how many forests and lakes we could make out from our distance, and we loved them. We had discovered them. We talked of them as "ours."

And then they took off. The liftoff of their spacecraft was visible to us. They would have sent earlier ones up if only to plant satellites, but this one was on our watch. When it reached our Taiwanese eyes and ears, it gave it a little bump. I was back at the controls, turning our ship around and following it. It was harrowing because of the speed. I felt like a cop on a dark city street with the killer escaping. Only to catch the thing was on my mind. But I couldn't. Halfway across our Milky Way the screen went dark.

One week later, while I was on my home computer ordering from a sale on dining accessories, a pair of very pleasant hazel eyes peered out at me from where, only a moment before, I had chosen six oval placemats in hemp. The eyes didn't blink. They looked directly into my—very shocked, I'd imagine—eyes as though considering a way through them into my brain. It was that eerie. I shut down the machine and texted Aldous, who was still at the institute. He came right over.

I turned my machine back on. My face, with the large face of Aldous beside me, filled the screen.

"I'm not on skype," I said. "Where's my home page? Why is my camera on?"

"You must have pushed a wrong button. I do that all the time."

"But I didn't."

Other things began to happen. It seemed as though I were being followed when I left the institute by a dark car that sped forward once I turned into my driveway, the garage door lifting slowly. I was missing mail. The thermostat setting for my air conditioner rose or fell at will. I felt like someone looking through binoculars into the window of a neighbor's house only to find out that neighbor had completely wired my house with video and listening devices.

It seemed I was the only one at the institute targeted. Was it because I'd been the one driving the Taiwanese spacecraft? We weren't sure.

"They're coming here," I told Aldous.

Now I was frightened. We all were.

. . .

That was five years ago.

In the intervening time, other entities and agencies became alert to the spacecraft. The military was first on it. But other SETI labs and astrophysics departments began tracking it. The press was now calling all the time. If they—whoever and whatever they might be—had hopped inside my computer, this information was known to them. I suspected they'd want to avoid landing in the midst of a mob, some of whom could be armed. All I was certain of was that they were close.

And I was right. They were.

What I would later learn was that, advanced as they were, as carefully as they had studied and copied us—learning our language and invading my computer in their efforts—they weren't infallible. They undershot their landing, coming to earth in a patch of ground in the Poconos, from which point they used a simulated smart phone to call a Lyft for a ride to the closest car dealership into which they carried a satchel of counterfeit bills, and this was how they ended up pulling into my driveway in Bridgewater, New Jersey, four of them, in matching white bodysuits, driving a pair of Corvettes.

Black-hair, olive skin, the one in front a ringer for a cousin of mine, they looked earthling. You understand what I'm saying here? The people I was meeting could have been my relatives. Ecstatic, I ran out to greet them. It was eleven on a Saturday morning. I had half a pot of coffee still hot. Did they drink coffee? Did they know what coffee was?

"Hello!" I was giddy with the newness of all this, with terror and with the feeling of being so very close to some enormous breakthrough. My heart rate—I was too overwhelmed to want to know how fast it was beating.

The one in the lead said, "I'm Ritchie," with a smile and an extended hand.

"Hello, Ritchie," I said and found I was laughing.

Yes, a full hand, four fingers and a thumb and a strong handshake. I was then introduced to Patty, Sam, and Max. The sweetness of them surprised me.

"Come in," I said, breathless. And before I knew it, I heard myself follow with, "It's been quite a trip. You must be hungry."

The four put their heads together and conversed while I texted Aldous. He arrived with Rain and three others from the institute, leaving the rest of the staff to man the place. Word would get out. We'd be inundated, but how quickly? How much time did we have alone with these four? There were tests to run. We'd need to get them to the institute for scans and cognitive tests and debriefings. How human were they? How did they think? I'd overheard them conversing, but their language gave no linguistic clues, a kind of guttural, melodic, burping noise, uptalking, like a reflux "I Feel Pretty."

If I couldn't make out the words, I certainly understood body language and tone. Here was my first indication of trouble. Ritchie was belching complaints to the other three, who were deferential. My heart went out to them as they dealt with him, for that's what they were doing, dealing with him, waiting him out, dodging his feints, slightly amused by it all, to be honest. And it was when Ritchie put his hand out in emphasis that I noticed an interstellar difference. The palms lacked lines. Those brackets on the underside of our finger joints were missing. I felt strangely rewarded seeing something, finally, that distinguished them and told me, yes, they were truly from another world. No psychic could read their futures by turning over their hands. Here was their mystery.

My dining room table was an old refectory board, and I covered it with bowls of salad and sliced meats, flatware (they were fascinated seeing a fork up close but knew how to use one). They ate much as anyone on earth, scarfing up chicken and tomatoes and cucumbers and baba ghanoush. They liked the iced tea.

When Aldous came in, he gave a little speech of welcome. He went on about his hope all these years for a connection.

The visitors looked shocked.

"What?" I asked. "What's wrong?"

"Your accent," Ritchie said to Aldous. "You don't talk like the rest of everyone."

"He's from Australia," I said.

This confused them.

"It's on the other side of our planet," I explained, "A different continent. The accent is different." I wondered if they felt they'd missed a detail in all their studies of us. In the lull that seemed to come from their embarrassment, I said, "Two hundred years ago, England, a large island, got rid of its criminals by sailing to the other side of the world and dumping them off. Aldous's ancestors were part of this."

"Criminals," Ritchie said.

The other three looked alarmed.

Aldous flushed beet red. I suppose it was possible to think a few billion in earnings and seven or eight generations should have redeemed him from that history. But my understanding was Aussie's were proud of those early forbears.

"That was ages ago," I said. "We can't go back in time, right? But they made it work for themselves. They survived." I almost added how very human this made them and stopped myself. Would this be considered an earth-centric bias? Not to mention how the aboriginal people had been treated. "What do you call yourselves? And your planet? What names?"

Some questioning belches went on among the four, and then Sam said, "Apex? Acme?" while Patty said, "Number one? You could say, 'The Best.'"

"You're besties," Rain said. "That's perfect."

Rain and Ben kept inquiring but in very gentle and friendly terms. I was thrilled at how they teased out whatever information they could. The Best was a crowded planet, we learned, but very clean. They had cleaned their air, lowered a rising temperature. We had to learn how.

"You came across space so fast," I said.

They looked at each other with expressions I can only call smug. "That's the rip," Sam said. "The only way to describe it in your language, I think."

"Miss the rip and we never hear from you again," Max said.

"We knew how to get into it," Sam said.

Aldous asked, "So we could find it on our end?"

Aldous was so excited he missed the glances they gave to his wrist-watch, the smart phone near his plate; our technology was viewed by them the way the rest of us might observe a horse and buggy.

I wondered how we would debrief these people. I also considered where these four would spend the night. There were no beds at the institute, and I realized we could hardly put them in cages. They should logically stay with me. I excused myself and ran upstairs, searching the linen closet for blankets. Noise on the street drew me to the window in the front bedroom. Local and cable news trucks were lumbering toward my house, behemoths, like something from the stone age. Then I noticed there were Corvettes parked here and there along the length of the block. I couldn't tell if anyone was in them. But I knew they didn't belong to my neighbors. I ran downstairs and signaled to Aldous. He excused himself and followed me.

We went into my home office. The room was on the other side of the kitchen and down a hall. It would give us privacy. He was nearly skipping, so happy was he.

"Molly. They're ours. They're here and we have them. And it's a dream. A dream come true."

"Something's wrong."

"No. The food is great. You're doing a wonderful job. Don't get into that negativity."

"Aldous. I have siblings who act more foreign. It's like these people read my mind."

"I know! They could be us. I want to go with them. When they go back. I'm serious!"

"Are they going back?"

He regarded me.

A shout of laughter came from the dining room.

"When you were upstairs," Aldous said, "they were saying 'Earth,' 'Earth,' and I hadn't realized what an ugly name that was."

"They're making fun of us."

"No they're not. They're fantastic. I think they like us."

"How do you think they got here? A rip? What does 'a rip' tell us? Nothing."

"Maybe they're a little bit more advanced. But, look, the Taiwanese craft made it to them."

"What race are they?"

"You mean . . . race?"

"They could be any race."

He considered this. "Yeah. They could be."

"These people are like three hundred years ahead of us. When everyone's all just kind of melded, in the same group."

"But that's good."

"It also means we're behind them. And they know it. We're backward."

"I'm not backward. How can you think that way?"

"They're laughing at us."

"You're paranoid."

"I'm trying to figure out how we get information from people who can run rings around us."

My attention was caught by a row of blinking lights outside the window. Helicopters. They were in the distance, flying low in the afternoon sky.

"We don't have much time."

"Why don't you accept them for how they are?" he asked.

"Because they studied us. They're just mimicking us. They could be bacteria in convincing costumes. They know more of our songs than I do."

Aldous's face struggled against disenchantment. He had the hurt expression billionaires get when they're not appreciated. "What should we do?" he asked.

"Get them to the institute. It's more secure."

He sighed. Slowly, he went out, and I bit my tongue, wanting to yell at him to hurry. There were sirens now. An arrival was imminent.

Before I was back in the dining room, there was a loud bang. The front door was thrown open, and everyone was coming in, a flood of people, scrambling to be first, to avoid being trampled. A TV camera knocked over a floor lamp and sent it crashing. There was yelling. A few people hollered questions—at whom? At all of us. A tsunami of humanity.

My concern was order. I pointed the cops toward the kitchen, the TV crews toward the living room. Keeping my voice level, I ascertained which group of fellow scientists were from which institute. The Caltech la-dee-dah bunch, I hustled to the deck outside. To an ancient man from Valparaiso University, I gave my chair, and Aldous offered him the spinach salad. As I turned, I noticed Rain sitting close to Ritchie. Their heads were together. The front door kept banging open, furniture kept crashing, voices were rising, questions about what the Field Institute was up to, about who or what had landed and who belonged to whom—the sense of possession this mob had for what went on around them. Meanwhile, I caught the look Ritchie was giving Rain and what he said, with his forefinger tracing her collarbone, was, "I think you're the smartest woman I ever met." It may have been caught on camera, too, because a boom mic swung very close to my head and then back and forth over the table. The police were raiding the refrigerator. We were almost out of food. Aldous was in the living room, talking to one of the cable news people. Ben was offering the last of the platters around.

Someone was missing. I realized I couldn't see the other three besties. Patty, Max, and Sam were nowhere in sight. From the sounds coming from upstairs, from the living room, from the deck, they could've been anywhere.

I hurried back to my office for some quiet. I needed to think. All the yelling was escalating into something nastier. My attention was caught by movement just outside the window. It was Patty, Max, and Sam. With stealth, I cracked open a lower pane. You blue jays, I thought. The harsh language I'd heard them speak earlier with Ritchie was now quite soft and musical as they spoke among themselves. Patty was rubbing her forehead back and forth against Sam's. Max was rubbing the top of Patty's shoulders. I wasn't sure what this meant in their world.

I opened the window a little more and said, "Psst. My friends."

The three looked up at me. The shift in their manner, in their facial expressions was frightening to me. To this day, I'm unable to describe it. The moment brought home to me the certainty I've always maintained that people, down deep, are unfathomable. They quickly smiled at me. I turned to head for the kitchen and the backdoor so I might join them.

As I left the room, I was approached by an officer of some security lineage, homeland or border or, possibly, a new agency of which I'd yet heard. About to ask if he'd like a cup of coffee, I realized his eyes had gone a bit dead. If you've ever been arrested, you know this look, disconnected from any feeling for you. The effect is maddening. I had no time for being arrested, and ducking, scurrying around, I slipped past him, squeezing into and through the crowd.

"Aldous," I called out, wanting him to come with me to the backyard and join the besties. I wasn't sure he could hear me above the din. I was caught behind a flock of news reporters until I pushed beyond them to a puzzle of theorists. They reversed my way, and I struggled forward. I found myself, finally, pressed against the living room window.

The driveway was empty.

"The Corvettes are gone."

The effect of this news was felt immediately by Ritchie and by those of us at the Field. That something momentous had happened brought a hush through the house. Rain suggested Patty, Sam, and Max might still be using the bathrooms.

"Maybe they went out for something," Ben said.

"Out for what," Ritchie said, his voice strained. "Potato chips and beer! No. They didn't go out for something."

"Are you familiar with the aria 'Nessun Dorma'?" I asked Aldous.

Unable to find his car and driver, he'd opted to ride shotgun in my Camaro before realizing it might be a bit tight for his frame.

"Molly, this connection has been my whole life. I feel everyone taking it away from me."

We were following Rain in her SUV. She drove with Ritchie beside her. Ritchie was guiding her back to the Poconos and the mother ship. It was already sundown. The cars lining up behind us, the gentle speed we were taking in order to keep everyone together as we headed toward the western sun, put me in mind of the pioneers wobbling along beside the Platte River and making their way out to Oregon. When I suggested this to Aldous, he snorted. Rain picked up speed at that point, and I kept up with her.

"They seem to be having a high old time of it," Aldous said.

I looked. Rain and Ritchie were talking with animation and laughing it up.

"I guess I'm not her type," Aldous said morosely. "Not that I'm allowed to find out," he said. "A man in my position can barely say hello to a woman."

"You say hello very nicely," I told him.

A large Aussie hand found my upper thigh. "At least there's you, then, eh?"

"Maybe we can deal with this later."

"Right." He withdrew the hand. After a few moments he asked, "Did you mean that about later?"

I glanced over at him. "We'll see."

"My ancestor was sent to Australia for stealing a handkerchief. The real story came down that he was stealing another man's wife. Now I risk crucifixion if I steal as much as a look at a woman. It's all come full circle. What's the value of talent then? Why make an effort? Used to be you racked up a few billion and people'd lay the world's goodies on you, you wouldn't need to ask. Not that I want to hurt anyone, but when did you Yanks get so bloody puritan?"

"You might want to look at it from the point of view of the women."

"Gladly, Molly, only I make too much money for it to do any good. I can't trust anyone. That's why I wanted a new world to live in. A real connection to someone."

"Do you think, maybe, it's all illusion? Maybe there is no connection anywhere? Maybe we're all just our own orb spinning out in the deep, thinking we hear someone else."

"Jesus. When I hired you, I wondered what made you tick. Now I'm glad I never found out."

When we pulled up behind Rain, she and Ritchie were getting out of her car. We followed them through woods onto a field. There was nothing but a burn mark in the grass the size of a snowboard.

"When your mates are back . . ." Aldous began.

"They're not coming back," Ritchie told him. "At least not to take me home."

"Were there others here?" I asked. "I saw Corvettes."

"I don't know," Ritchie said. "I kept trying to get information out of them, but they wouldn't tell me a whole lot."

We took another path out to Rain's SUV and drove off just as the other cars and trucks that had been following us braked and parked behind my Camaro. I turned to see the crowd that had filled my house now disembarking to trace our footprints into the woods.

We drove to the car dealership. There, in a line, were the Corvettes that had been in my driveway and a few others, the very ones I'd seen on the street.

"They're gone," Ritchie said.

"Can you reach them?" Aldous asked. "Communicate? Tell them to come back? Maybe they got confused and didn't mean to leave without you?"

Ritchie explained that there was another planet like ours but in the opposite direction from the Best. "If that tin can you launched had kept going, you'd have found it. But it's packed too. Earth appears to have a lot of room."

"They came just to dump you off?"

"I'm not clean enough for them."

Aldous's face grew a bright red. "We'll not be made a new penal colony, mate. We won't abandon you. Never."

"Never," Rain said. And in Rain's voice was affection.

. . .

Which was how I came to be maid of honor at Rain and Ritchie's wedding. *Coupling* might be the better word for their union since the ceremony, lovely with vows expressed between two rows of potted hydrangeas, wasn't registered. It was held in the anteroom of the institute. Ritchie turned out to be quite the traditionalist; he asked Aldous to preside, saying something about Aldous being the "captain of the ship." Rain confided that she was looking toward her wedding night with some trepidation.

"I'm sure it'll be fine."

"You know all their behavior that's been exactly like ours? That's not how they are."

"This is what I was trying to find out."

"I'll let you know what I discover."

"Rain, you don't have to go to bed with a man to find out what he's really like."

"Of course I do."

"I don't want you getting into trouble. Don't do this."

But the next day, Ritchie from another world took the conflicted Rain to have and to hold. No one since the Montagues and the Capulets observed a couple with as much angst as Aldous and I did.

In the meantime, I tried to find the besties' spacecraft as it sped toward home. Aldous came in and sat in Rain's empty chair.

"Don't bother," he told me. "Apparently, they think we're their dump. I no longer want anything to do with them."

"I hope that's possible. I have a feeling we'll be seeing more of them."

"Not me. I'm closing the institute."

"But this is your life's work. It's your baby."

"The military and the other institutes want to interview me. So does the press. By the time I'm done with all of them, we should have shuttered the place in an orderly fashion. Rain will be back next week. I don't want to pull the job out from under her while she's on her honeymoon. I'm sorry, Molly. I'll write you a good letter of recommendation. Didn't you want to work on some disease? Now's your chance."

"What will you do?"

"I realize I haven't seen enough of my own planet. I'd like to. Maybe take some pictures." The remark had no joy in it.

I confess I had little joy myself at that moment.

Then Rain didn't show up for work.

Aldous put his arm around me as we left the crematorium at the end of her funeral.

I told him, "I know it was Ritchie."

"I think so too."

I nodded to his driver and climbed into the back of the car. As I explained to Aldous, Ritchie had no presence, no identification, no citizenship. No one would suspect or find him. Since we were responsible for his being here, we were obligated to track him down.

"He could be anywhere. How would we find him?"

"What if he didn't just murder Rain? What if killing people was his crime. There'll be others. We go at it methodically. Piece by piece until we get the whole picture. Then we close in."

I sensed a spark of life in him. It would be activity that suited both of us—a scientist needs a puzzle, and a billionaire needs a cause.

We began our search in cities among ordinary people, something I think did Aldous a world of good. Sometimes, on a grocery line, say, or on a subway platform, we'd nudge each other: Was that Ritchie? Ritchie stepping into a car. Ritchie ducking into a stairwell. Should we try upstate? Should we look again through the Poconos? We thought we'd spotted him on a ferry and, later, in a bookstore.

We went farther afield, expanding our territory, an eye on wedding venues since Ritchie by himself might need what he surely imagined he'd have gotten from Rain: care and shelter.

For a long time, we searched as though our lives depended on it. We became as one in many ways. Certainly, I'd never seen Aldous as exuberant or as free. People who knew me said I'd "bloomed." As long as there was hope—Was that Ritchie in the cereal aisle? That's him running down the hill, no?—we were happy. But in time, I felt both of us winding down. We'd simply been at it too long. Discouragement is a slow toxin.

The day came when Aldous sat ponderously on my sofa and said, "I want to go home."

"Do you need a ride?"

"Of course not. I meant home to Australia."

He had many houses, all of them in North America. The sentiment surprised me. In the meantime, my house had never recovered from the chaos of the crowds teeming in.

So I told him, "I'm coming with you."

He nodded.

"You're not really giving up the chase, are you?" I asked him.

"I never give up," he said, truculent. There was something very boyish about Aldous. And yet, I'd never seen him look so old.

There was staff galore to get his plane ready and pack his clothes. He paced while I threw a few things into my carry-on. I worried about the sadness that only deepened in both of us during the very long trip.

"We never got the information on interstellar velocity," I said while we were still over the endless Pacific.

He smiled then. "We could use some of it, couldn't we?"

Was it his home? The streets of his childhood had been long transformed. There was no evidence of his early years—at least not until we happened into a pub one night. Aussie heaven I thought, pints all around and an impromptu band wailing away about a convict ship. Within the folds of that evening, Aldous seemed to find his younger self.

"I wanted," he began telling me. He had trouble finding the words. "I wanted to get out. When I was growing up here. I wanted to go, I don't know, somewhere. Get myself out and go—"

A man asking for a handout was in front of us.

"Don't," I told Aldous and tried to shoo the man away.

22

But Aldous had cash and some change. He was already offering it. The man's palm opened out to receive the money, a palm thrust under a light and noticeable for lacking lines, for no joint brackets, for the fingertips smooth as paper. We looked up as the fingers closed around the money.

Ritchie started, recognizing us. He turned and hurried into the crowd.

I hollered, "That was him!"

Aldous was already up. Our hoots and yells blended into the music cracking the air. We were back on the chase.

"We'll get him," I hollered and felt Aldous's hand close around mine.

Outside, the air held a brine and fish scent. It was dark. There were people milling about. Aldous's car and driver were at the curb.

He waved them off and asked me, "Which way?"

We ran toward the lights and the crowd along a main boulevard. I felt my heart racing—talk about velocity.

"Will we find him?" he asked me, excitement lifting his voice.

"We will," I told him. "We will."

Escape

YEARS LATER, WHEN she was very old, Kate could still recall the hour she waited in that heat for her cousin, Vincent, to appear. She'd counted on a family resemblance to spot him and, finally, from the far end of the pier, came the Farley nose on a tall, slim gent.

"Vincent?" she called.

He turned to her. Tommy, her brother, was waiting just beyond the crowd in a borrowed car, a nice one.

On their way across town, Kate saw the fold along the collar of Vincent's shirt open and close like a long, thin mouth where the fabric had worn out. His neck was bright white. From a recent haircut, she figured, and her heart went out to him. There, when he turned his face and she studied the sharp bones, the dark eyes, she'd have to say he was handsome. And his manner was winning: deferential, full of smiles. He might do all right for himself. She wanted to judge him the way New York would, brutally; and, yes, she decided, he had a chance here. Her concern on first getting his letter (Who is Vincent?) saying he'd be emigrating (Emigrating for what? The economy had collapsed) was the possibility he'd end up a burden.

"When Kate and I came over," Tommy was telling him, a stutter slightly bouncing his speech, "it was boom times."

"Nineteen twenty-five," Kate said. "Ten years here. We're old-timers."

Vincent turned from taking in the sights and regarded them. "You was only kids."

"And dumb as dirt," Kate laughed. "We had to scramble."

"You needn't worry," Tommy told Vincent. "It looks like everyone here is on a bread line, but keep your chin up."

Brother and sister shared a two-bedroom flat, a walk-up, the living room furnished with rescued pieces from the curbs of better neighborhoods. To see their cousin look around with admiration had Kate share a glance with Tommy.

"The sofa is really a daybed," Kate said. "Plenty of room for you."

When Tommy asked Vincent what he thought he might do, he said, "Anything above ground."

"You've had enough of the mines?"

"The whole way across the Atlantic, I was coughing coal dust. I think I was part of the propulsion." He was grinning, making a joke of it, but a moment later, he said, "God Christ, I never thought I'd get out of there at all."

It was through Tommy—offering suggestions, explaining things— that Vincent put together a plan. In the borrowed car, he went to Canal Street, where he loaded up the trunk with household goods. He went up north into Westchester County, the sticks. Door to door, he sold his pots and pans and needles and pins. In those days, a lot of housewives were stuck without a way to travel into town. They might only need the simplest of things.

When he came in from his first day of selling, it was very late.

"I saved some dinner for you," Kate said.

"Thanks be to God. I'm completely starved."

"You didn't stop for a bite?"

"I didn't dare," he laughed.

"We'll have to pack a lunch for you next time," Kate said and waited, thinking he'd tell her how he'd managed.

He didn't tell her anything. In time, she'd realize the days that went very well made him the most circumspect.

"Like a poker player," she told Tommy.

Later, when she was in bed, Kate heard coins being counted in the living room, the sound close to musical.

"I had to smile," Kate told Tommy. "Did he think we might take some? Or steal his business? Dish towels and vegetable scrapers? How much do you think he's getting for them?"

"I haven't the foggiest. I mean, the very idea that there's people buying the stuff. It's bloody wonderful."

"Do you think he'll stay with us long?"

"He'll get tired of that daybed I expect."

"Good," she said, and Tommy laughed.

They were talking after supper, alone, the way they'd learned to confide in each other years ago when they'd been desperate to leave the old country, to escape.

"What if he never leaves?"

"We'll charge him rent," she laughed.

But the speed with which Vincent found his own place, bought a used car, and eloped with an American girl took the brother and sister by surprise. And then the baby. Seven months later, a healthy baby girl was born, Susan.

"He was busier than I thought," Kate said.

It wasn't until the baby was christened that Kate and Tommy met Vincent's new wife and realized why she hadn't been brought around sooner.

"Cold," Kate described Margaret later to some friends. "That kind of blonde, you know? Looking down her nose at you. Rude she was. I said I was so glad to meet her. But she cut me dead."

The baby was cradled in Vincent's arms. Cooing and gurgling, Susan spent the day with her daddy rocking her and, at one point, singing softly to her. Vincent carried on so much that Kate began to think he was compensating for the mother. Margaret stood off to one side with her eyelids half closed as though she'd found all of them unbearable.

There had been no other family. Kate suspected grievance over the shotgun marriage and went to Margaret, her hand on the young mother's arm, persistent and certain she'd found the key to this woman's behavior.

"She's beautiful. Your Susan. You must be so proud."

Margaret recoiled. And the look she gave Kate.

"Like I was dirt," Kate said to her friends. Her friends had been following the Vincent story. "Like my slip was showing and I needed a wash."

Just as well, she consoled herself, since there'd be little time to see them and keep up any friendship. They moved well north of the city. Kate placed them with the rarely seen—Christmas card people—and was happy to be free of them.

About four years later, Kate was on her way home from work and found Vincent standing in front of her apartment house, coming to attention when he saw her. He was ashen. She thought he might be dying.

"No one answered your buzzer," he said.

"Tommy's full time now."

"I need your help," he said.

"Come in."

Before taking off her hat and gloves she poured him a drink.

"It's Susan," he said. "Margaret ran away. And she took the baby." He couldn't finish the glass. He put it down with a shaking hand. "She took my child with her. My Susan's gone."

He told her how Margaret, at home with a newborn, had made herself busy. She had a sewing machine and taught herself to make men's ties. "There were some businesses opening up where we are, and she'd go into them selling her neckties. Places where the men had to wear ties." He looked about to weep.

Taking a page from Vincent's enterprise, Kate thought. Homemade ties, if at all done well, would have found a market given the price of a store-bought one, and more to the point, the men who needed ties would've loved the sight of Margaret, something Margaret would have known. They would have bought as many as they could from a woman who looked like Margaret. Well, well.

"She ran off with an office manager. They have Susan. They took Susan from me. The court says I'm on the road all week and can't take care of her. I want you to help me. You could help me get her back."

"Oh, Vincent," Kate said, thinking she could do little but sympathize.

"You know how to type. That's what they want. Letters to the authorities."

"But those are for a court. I'm not sure I'd know how to do that."

"They say I'm an itinerant," he said, "and they want the baby in a stable home."

"Where does Margaret provide a stable home? Doesn't she sell door to door?"

"Not anymore. She stays home with Susan."

"But she ran off with another man. While she was married to you."

"It doesn't matter about Margaret," he said. "It's the baby. Susan is mine. I come home now, and she's not there."

Kate could imagine Margaret calling on businessmen, showing her wares. What a setup. And why, for that matter, had she been making men's ties? Why not aprons or kitchen towels? Sashaying in front of men, what was she thinking? And Vincent losing his daughter. Kate thought if anyone could write a letter to move the scales of justice to where they balanced, it was herself.

"What do you need?"

"Testaments to my character," he said miserably. "That I could take care of my own child."

"Shouldn't be impossible."

Tommy helped her carry home a used typewriter to work on what she called "The Case." By dragging two floor lamps to either side of the table, she could keep at it late into the night. The temptation was to go to bed. She was tired by the end of the day. And Vincent should have hired a lawyer to do much of what she was doing. But she only had to remember Margaret's treatment of her at the baptism, and she'd be good for another two or three hours, typing away into the night.

She had Tommy read everything she wrote.

"You've the gift," he said. "Will you have a career with this sort of work?"

"If I do, it'll be thanks to Margaret," she laughed.

"Will they let him keep the door-to-door business?" Tommy asked her.

"No."

"Terrible. He's been at it a good while. I'd say he enjoys it."

"He needs to be at home. What kind of business can you do at home?"

"A hotel?"

"With a wishing well," she sang.

"It would do for him, though. He'd be there all day."

She considered it. Shaking her head, she told him, "You'd need a sink and toilet in every room. And a steady stream of customers coming in, or you're bunched."

"How about a boarding house?"

They were eating dinner buffet style, as they called it, since the dining room table was covered with papers.

She pointed her fork at him. "A boarding house might be perfect."

There was a boarding house two blocks away and it was full of theater people. She imagined they'd be interesting people to be around.

Vincent liked the idea. Kate drove up from the city to meet with him and look at properties for sale. When they reached Ossining, they saw it. A big porch and a dark, overhanging roof, solid looking and freshly painted a bright yellow. The price seemed right.

"Don't look eager," Kate said softly to Vincent.

Tommy came up to inspect it. He went through the basement and in and out of closets with a flashlight. It was in fine shape, on a main thoroughfare. And it was already in operation as a boarding house; there were already tenants.

She had anticipated a lot of furniture, chintz, and colorful theatrical posters, but there was simply a brown sofa in the main room downstairs with a wooden coffee table. Vincent could make it homey, dress it up a little. Near the front door was a frame holding the room rates. Six bedrooms. At those rents, you could bank a bit of money after expenses.

A few things that caused her to grin: a wall lamp over the table in the kitchen with a chain pull. It looked so delicate in that big room. A child could do homework under it. She made a note to refer to it in another letter to the court.

And off the first floor, like a separate house, was a generous suite of rooms, private, for the owner and his family. The child wouldn't be in the main part of the house at all. Vincent would have to hire a housekeeper, of course, and that woman's presence would be good for the little girl.

"This could work," Kate said.

"I don't know. Will they want too much for it?" Vincent said.

"But this would do," Kate said. "You and Susan would have plenty of room in the private area. There's three big bedrooms back there and a nice bathroom all to yourselves."

He talked about getting the price knocked down, and Kate loaned him enough to secure the mortgage. And then they went to court. Margaret gave them a good fight. The man she'd run off with hired a lawyer.

"We tried," Kate told Tommy. "I never thought we had it in the bag. Taking a child from its mother."

But when the decision came, the child was given to her father. Vincent was given full custody. They were so surprised they hardly had time to celebrate.

"You're a miracle worker," he said to Kate. "I don't know how you pulled it off."

She felt again Margaret's effect on her, Margaret and her cold shoulder. So there, she might have said to Margaret. Take that, you!

"You could marry and have a child, like Vincent," Kate said to Tommy. "Then they'd give you a deferment. You wouldn't have to go."

"I don't mind doing my bit," Tommy said. "I should have enlisted after Pearl Harbor."

He was in uniform. Pleased with himself, she thought, the shiny buttons, the stiff crease in the pants. Looking spiff. Seeing him off at the pier brought back to Kate the memory of their escape years ago from the back of beyond; Tommy charming the shopkeeper out from behind her grocer's counter, chatting her up like she was some vision for him, his gentle stutter like he'd been enchanted, and indeed, the lady went off with him, showing him some bit of memento she'd hung on the wall, her back to Kate, because Tommy knew—Kate was certain—that Kate could steal; days on the road after their food ran out and Tommy describing what it would be like seeing a boat in the harbor. It would be waiting just for Kate. His kindness, his nervous stomach, his obvious gallantry. What would become of him? Like sending a show horse or a Steinway grand into battle, they should only take thick-skinned lugs.

The young man she'd been seeing—thick-skinned or no—followed Tommy and so did the many young men who'd previously marched down the streets in early morning on their way to work. Had she thought to visit Vincent and his young daughter, she would've had a time trying to get there; there was gas rationing. Still, she kept in touch, sent cards and, when she had the money, little toys for the child.

When the war was over, she phoned Vincent. She needed a favor. Tommy was back but in poor health. His nerves were shot, the consequence being his stutter was intense. Sometimes she could hardly make out what he was saying. His old boss hired him back for clerical work in their Ossining office. Could he live with Vincent and Susan in the boarding house?

"I'm engaged," she told him. "We'll be moving across the river into Jersey. I don't want Tommy living alone." If someone in the family had an eye out for him, she'd feel better.

"Of course," Vincent said.

In the early years of her marriage, it was Tommy who traveled to her. The baby years. Four toddlers and a late pregnancy, number five, kept her at home. Tommy came into Jersey carrying a bag full of children's books or toys. With only the kids around him, his stutter abated. There were afternoons when he was there that Kate slept like the dead.

It was a dozen years before Kate drove up to the boarding house. So much time had passed, she nearly got lost on the way. The whole area was built up, confusing her. She missed a sign lowering the speed limit and was pulled over and given a ticket. When she arrived at the place, Tommy was at the door to meet her, his suitcase beside him.

"A cop pulled me over," she said, trying to laugh. "A policeman!"

He lifted his face, trying to say something, the struggle causing his eyes to close, his chin to shake.

"I know," she laughed. "I was probably going too fast."

As Tommy grabbed his bag to go, Vincent called to them from the kitchen. "I have cake for you."

She followed Tommy to the back of the house, past the common room still with the brown sofa and the wooden coffee table. Nothing had been altered in all the years since she'd first seen it.

"Good God," she murmured.

The kitchen was the same too. Well, she told herself, if it ain't broke. She took the chair Vincent pulled out for her. Tommy sat across from her.

"And," Vincent said with ceremony, "I made a fresh pot of coffee. I know you like strong coffee, Kate."

Strong it was and welcome. She was tired. The cake was almost pure sugar, painful to eat, but she thanked Vincent, who remained in motion.

It was that day, as she sat eating the too-sweet cake, that she began to realize how energetic her cousin was. He let her know he did the repair work on the place himself and then ticked off a number of fix-it items that he'd taken care of over the years, including the replacement of a few shingles on the roof. The cooking was his, but he loved cooking, he said.

"You won't save money unless you cook the meals yourself. A person you pay to do it will never economize."

About to ask him if he had any help at all, she looked up as Susan filled the doorway.

"Susan," Vincent called out. "Do you know your Aunt Kate?"

Kate stared at the girl. A pair of eyes like Margaret's glanced at her without expression. Susan was grown.

The years flying by, the adjustment from infant to young woman, gave Kate the sensation of her soul tripping and falling down a flight of stairs. Susan was a teenager. And she was a type Kate considered American, as in foreign to her, beyond her knowing. All Kate's efforts at fitting in came a cropper around these tall and self-possessed young women. Age and position were the only way to handle them.

"Sit down here," Kate told her. "Let me have a look at you."

But the girl remained in the doorway as though she were giving Kate the rare gift of her patience.

Vincent called out "Susan" this and "Susan" that (She might want a piece of cake. She didn't.) as though he were a fan and she some movie star. And Susan with that look. Like Margaret. Cold.

"I just got a speeding ticket," Kate said and rummaged in her purse for it. "Wait'll you see this!" Wanting to read it, wanting her attention somewhere besides the girl, absently, she pulled the chain on the little lamp above the table. As she bent to read the crabbed script, the light went off. She looked up to find Vincent turning away from the table.

"You don't need that in God's daylight," he said, like something he'd said a million times before. "Not like you're doing surgery there." He was already across the room.

Kate looked over at Susan still in the doorway and the girl seemed to soften a bit.

"And you're in high school?" Kate asked.

"Susan," Vincent said from the other side of the room, "is a junior in high school."

"And what," she asked the girl, ignoring Vincent, "do you want to be, you know, later? What is it you're studying?" She smiled hard at Susan, sick of this place already and wanting to take Tommy and leave.

"Susan," Vincent called out, "has a birthday this week. You must have forgotten."

Kate saw that Tommy had finished his cake. Quickly, she brought the plates and cups to the sink. "A long drive ahead," she said, laughing lightly. "Oh, Susan, it was wonderful to see you. All grown up!"

Cold like her mother, Kate thought when she passed her in the doorway, the girl recoiling slightly, backing away. No hope of an embrace or a chance for Kate to possibly take her aside and see how she really was.

On the way home, Kate asked Tommy about her. "She's fine," Tommy said. "She's a job in town b . . . b . . . b. . . ."

"Babysitting?" She waited through an uncomfortable silence. Then she said, "The next time I come, maybe we'll bring her down with us to meet the kids and have an outing. My girls could take her under their wing."

But two days after that conversation, Susan turned sixteen and left the boarding house forever. She made a beeline for her mother. She packed up and moved out and never had anything to do with her father again.

"She knew where Margaret was?" Kate asked Vincent.

"Margaret shadowed her. I don't know when they got together," Vincent said. "So much for legal custody. Once Susan turned sixteen, I couldn't stop her. It was a conspiracy."

Kate didn't ask if he wanted her back. He'd spoiled her rotten as far as Kate could tell. Maybe the mother could do something with her.

. . .

One Saturday during the early seventies, Kate arrived at the boarding house with her youngest, Jeannie. Jeannie had driven the rental
truck. They were moving Tommy into Kate's house. Retired, his health
deteriorating, he had agreed to let Kate take care of him.

"I wish he'd met someone," Kate said when Jeannie pulled the truck
into the narrow driveway. "Tommy should have married and had a
family. They'd be there for him now."

"You know he's a homosexual."

"What?"

"Uncle Tommy. You know that, right?"

"What are you saying? He got hurt in the war."

"Jesus, Mom."

"Your Uncle Tommy came home from the war with that stutter."

"Fine. I know that. But he is also a homosexual."

"My brother . . ." Kate said, but realized she knew he was a homosexual. She simply didn't know she knew.

"It's all right!" Jeannie yelled. "It doesn't matter. I was just saying."

As Kate listened to one of Jeannie's exasperated sighs, a worry began to stitch its way through her: she had assumed all along that the
boarding house was full of theater types. Not that there couldn't be
lovely people of some other occupation staying there. But she couldn't
remember seeing any. There was never anyone around. Tommy was
always so eager to go.

As she expected, Tommy was at the door to greet them, his luggage
already in the hallway. Just beyond was the communal parlor, the brown
sofa and the coffee table. Why, she wondered, did Vincent never think
to update that room? Well, it wasn't her boarding house.

Jeannie, after giving her Uncle Tommy a hug, picked up his luggage
and carried it out to the truck. Kate moved toward the private family
quarters, hoping he hadn't acquired anything too heavy for them to
manage. Vincent was out somewhere that day and wasn't around to
help.

Tommy gestured her toward the stairs.

"What? You're upstairs!" she said. "I thought you were living in the family rooms."

"N . . . n . . . no," Tommy said. "T . . . t . . . top of the stairs."

She wanted Vincent in front of her. She wanted to tell him off. What were you thinking? Tommy helped you when you first came over. You couldn't give him a room with the family? But Vincent wasn't home. Right, Kate thought. And I could have asked. I could have made a point of the details years ago. It hadn't crossed her mind that he wouldn't bring Tommy in as family. It never occurred to her.

Tommy's bedroom was small and centered at the top of the stairs. There was a single bed with a dark headboard and a matching wooden dresser. No window.

"Are these yours?" she asked Tommy about the furniture.

He said no.

"So that's something we won't have to carry," she said and tried to laugh.

A cell, she thought, the room was like a prison. Through the wall came voices from the next room. The language sounded like gargling. What country? She had no idea. But they were men speaking. And nothing theatrical in the voices. Too far north, she realized, for people trying to get on a Broadway stage.

"Who boards here?" she asked and waited through the noise from Jeannie outside, thundering open the back of the truck.

Tommy finally managed to say, "Construction."

She fingered the blankets and the thin counterpane. "The linens stay?"

He nodded.

A box was on a chair. She filled it with the few things remaining, winter sweaters and an old hat. A feeling of defeat swamped her.

"Oh Lordy," she murmured.

It wasn't possible that he'd been living like this all the times she came by and met him waiting for her at the front door, the two of them excited to be off. Tommy unable to speak much of anything and she talking, talking, so relieved and so happy to have her brother beside her. She could finally unburden herself of all the minutiae that had her racing from morning to night.

"Oh Tommy," she said.

She spotted, among books, a cache of papers held in a rubber band. They were made out to Tommy. Each showed a date and a dollar amount with Vincent's signature. They were receipts for room rent.

"You were paying?" She studied the papers, realizing the rental amount was the full rate for the room. "Why was he charging you?"

"He'd charge the squirrels for the n . . . n . . . n . . . nuts, if he. . . ."

She nodded. The reason he didn't invite Tommy into the private quarters where he'd stay for free. She might have found this out earlier. Could have asked. "What a cheap son of a bitch."

The smartass remark when he'd turned off the light while she'd tried to read her speeding ticket. And the damn cake—plenty left over since no one could eat it. Could he not have given her an actual meal after she'd driven so far? As much as a sandwich?

"Miserable cheap bastard."

It dawned on her that he'd had the down payment to purchase the boarding house, but he'd taken the no-interest loan she'd offered and kept his own money safely compounding. And no housekeeper. Ever. The little girl missing her mother. Kate remembered the careful notes of each coin hitting a coin as he counted them in the old apartment late into the night. He was a miser. Not charming at all. The charm was fake, a means to make money. What Margaret had found herself married to.

"Margaret knew," she said. "She must have known about him before we even met her. Margaret knew before the baptism."

Tommy's eyebrows rose. He looked at Kate.

"All the papers I typed. All that work. So he could take the child." For a moment, she held on to the top of the bureau. "Jesus."

She heard Jeannie coming into the house. Quickly, not wanting her daughter to see this room, she gathered up the boxes with Tommy and hurried downstairs.

"Right," she said to Jeannie, dumping some of the stuff into the girl's waiting arms. "Now. Here we go then."

"Mom, let me ..."

"Hurry up!"

Outside, she tore the keys from her daughter's hand and climbed into the truck, which was almost as empty as when they'd arrived. A quick glance to see Tommy settled in beside Jeannie and she took off, driving as fast as she could, trying to outrun Margaret.

"Mom," Jeannie said. "I was going to drive this thing."

"We grew up poor," Kate yelled at her. "Tommy and me. I once got a pair of cast-off shoes for Christmas. That was the only Christmas present I ever got in my life. They were too big for me, but I was thrilled. Thrilled."

"N...n...n...now."

"Mom, you're speeding!"

"People treated us like dirt. I thought we'd never get out of there. It's not my fault."

The near-empty truck shuddered and tilted over the blacktop, back tires thumping like doom.

Jeannie braced herself with her hands against the dashboard, yelling, "Everybody in my family is crazy."

Speeding didn't help. Margaret was all over the place. Like an apparition, the sky full of the young mother, baby in one arm and the other extending an open box of men's neckties, looking for her way out.